FIFTY
COFFEE
BREAK
SHORT
STORIES

with a twist
or two!

Brian Humphreys

Published in 2012 by FeedARead Publishing

British Library C.I.P.

A CIP catalogue record for this title is available from the British Library.

Cover design and photographs, courtesy of
A1 Camera Club: www.a1cameraclubweston.co.uk

Also by Brian Humphreys
The Accidental Christian
African Adventures of a Born-Again Atheist

Dedication

To my wife Irene

She is the sounding board to all of my writing. She is my number one critic, she doesn't pull her punches, and I have the bruises to prove it.

Most time she listens attentively, sometimes she falls asleep, and sometimes she waits patiently until I have finished reading a new story or poem before saying: 'When are you going to start decorating the living room like you promised me five years ago?'

We have been married for over 40 years, and in my book, she can do no wrong, but in real life; now that's a different matter entirely.

Contents

Contents – continued

Contents – continued

Snippets from the book:

African Adventures of a Born-Again Atheist

Introduction

From biblical times to the Bristol riots of 2011, each of these stories take you into a different world, and as you travel in time, so you travel around the world, from darkest Africa to Buckingham Palace, from a Butlins holiday camp to Hell (and some people would argue that they are one and the same).

Stories vary in length from 50 to 2,500 words, so whether you have five minutes or half an hour, pour yourself a drink, put your feet up, and enjoy over 50 short stories containing more twists than a Chubby Checker concert.

From the innocent question 'Mummy, where do babies come from?' to the search for eternal youth: join royalty, children, teenagers, mums, dads, grandparents, vampires and superheroes as they face the stress and strains of everyday life. Love affairs begin and end, relationships are laid bare, and sometimes, blood is spilled.

Romance, horror, an abundance of humour, and possibly the world's worst practical joke idea (page 109), are all here in these reflections of normal (and abnormal) life.

You may guess a few story endings, but I will surprise you, often. ENJOY.

Brian Humphreys, author

Don't be Daft, Grandad

Short listed: Somerset Short Story Competition 2011

Thank God for the Sabbath, thought Angus McLoud, guiding an electric toothbrush over the remnants of his 60-year-old teeth. Downstairs, the telephone rang four times before his wife Rose answered. She's slowing down, he noted; perhaps I should trade her in for a younger model.

Her voice boomed up the stairs. 'It's Steven. Can we babysit our grandkids?'

'No! It's the Sabbath, a day of rest, and if it's good enough for Jesus, it's good enough for me.' Jungle telegraph was the main form of communication in the McLoud household.

'Your dad said that's fine, we'll be round in 30 minutes.'

Rose was already in the car, checking her hair and make-up, when Angus slumped behind the wheel.

'Where to?' There it was again, short-term memory loss.

'To collect the twins.'

Angus started the engine. 'This time, be firm with them, they need discipline. Kids can sense fear and weakness right away.'

'They're six-year-old twins; there's no need for a military exercise.' Rose noticed shaving foam behind his left ear. 'Are you OK to drive?'

Angus gave her his new and improved death-stare, level five.

As he drove, Rose studied his profile. He had hair befitting a mad professor, had started to behave like one, and was showing early signs of dementia.

'Can't this thing go any faster?' she asked.

'It's not a thing. It's a Skoda Octavia, and I'm doing 33 in a 30 limit.'

'So that's why my face is distorted.'

'No, that's inbreeding, dear.'

'Mum's worried about you,' said his son, as they fitted booster seats in the back of the car.

'You know what she's like, son, I'm fine.' Angus's headaches had been getting worse, but that was between him and his cerebral cortex.

He gave the twin boys high fives. 'Come on, kids, to the Batmobile.'

'Don't be daft, Grandad,' they shouted, 'the Batmobile's black, not green.'

Angus strapped them into their seats, his crucifix swinging from his neck.

'Grandad, why do you wear a chain around your neck?' asked Robert, the older twin by three minutes.

'In case he gets lost,' said Rose.

'Just remember, kids, God loves you - but he loves me best.'

'Don't be daft, Grandad,' said Robert, 'God loves us all the same.'

Grandson Thomas joined in. 'Grandad, where did you find God?'

'I didn't find him; *he* found me.'

'Where were you hiding, Grandad?' asked Thomas.

'See what you've started?' said Rose.

'I was hiding under Grandma's thumb.'

'Don't be daft, Grandad,' the twins shouted, 'you're too big to hide under Grandma's thumb.'

Angus eased the car out into traffic. 'Remember, Rose, encourage good behavior, and if that fails, we'll use handcuffs.'

'Don't be daft, Grandad,' shouted Thomas. 'You haven't got any handcuffs.'

Robert loved policemen and police cars. 'I wish I had some handcuffs.'

'One day, I'll get you some.'

'Wow, thanks, Grandad.'

'I wish you wouldn't encourage him, Angus.'

'Blame our son, don't blame me. I told him to name his son Angus, but did he listen? No, he called him Robert.'

'And what's wrong with the name Robert?'

'Shorten the name Robert and you get Bobby or Rob! No wonder he's obsessed with the police.'

'My name is Thomas John,' said Robert's twin brother with pride.

'There you are, Rose. Thomas shortens to Tommy, and he loves soldiers and tanks. Still it could have been worse,' he continued, 'instead of Thomas John, they could have named him John Thomas, or worse still, "Willie".'

The boys giggled at the word 'willie'.

Rose shook her head. 'So, is it the name Angus that makes you behave like a silly cow?'

The combination of loud mooing noises from the backseat and the flea in his ear distracted Angus and he drove through a red light.

Poor concentration, thought Rose, another sign.

'Grandma, will you buy me some chocolates and Coke?' asked Robert.

'And me, Grandma,' said Robert, not wishing to be left out.

'Of course,' replied Rose, happy to at least buy some affection. 'Angus, please stop at the supermarket.'

In a child's voice, Angus said, 'Will you buy me some chocolates as well?' As they neared the supermarket, he pointed out of the car window, 'Look boys, a BMW LS rear-engine Coupe. You don't see those every day; they only built 1,730.'

After finding a parking space, Angus addressed his young lieutenants. 'OK, troops, best behaviour in the supermarket, please.' Inside the store, his grandchildren ignored his words and grabbed handfuls of chocolates, safe in the knowledge that Rose would not tell them off. She led them to the checkout.

'Can I enter your PIN?' shouted Thomas, attracting the attention of everyone within earshot.

'Of course, it's 1-9-6-6.'

Angus shook his head and tried to look like he wasn't with them as Rose, holding both the grandchildren's hands, followed him into the car park. He scanned the rows of vehicles.

'Can't you remember where we parked?' asked Rose.

'Look, a boy with red hair. Only one percent of people are natural redheads, you know.'

'Don't change the subject. Have you lost it again?'

'Rose, how many times have I actually lost the car?'

'Do you mean in England, or worldwide?'

'Hang on a minute, you can't count Portugal. That was a hire car in a foreign car park and I was wearing sunglasses. I'm talking about *our* car.'

'Not counting Portugal, I make it seven.'

'Well, that's not bad for a 60-year-old. It works out once every eight or nine years.'

'Except for one important fact, dear: you've only been driving for two years.'

'OK, that's a fair point, but am I the only one here with two eyes and a memory?'

'It's over there, Grandad,' said Thomas.

The attack was over in seconds. Whilst helping his grandchildren into the back of the car, Angus suffered excruciating pain across the back of his head. But this was no violent headache; it was a blow from behind by an opportunist thief, who grabbed Rose's handbag and quickly ran away. The children screamed at the sight of blood seeping from Grandad's head.

Clutching her grandchildren, Rose said scathingly, 'Shouldn't a great military leader have been watching his rear?'

Much to Robert's delight, two policemen appeared. 'Did anyone see what happened?'

Someone said, 'Perhaps it's on CCTV?'

'Why would it be on children's television?' asked a confused Angus. He mumbled two more words before falling unconscious: 'BMW, redhead.'

After seven days in a coma, Angus opened his eyes and slowly but surely, remembered every detail. Rose shouting out her PIN number, the chocolates, the youth with red hair, the blow on the head, and the unmistakeable sound of a BMW LS Coupe starting up as he lay on the ground.

Sitting beside him, checking her hair and make-up, Rose was trying to remember where the insurance policies were kept.

'Where are my chocolates, Rose? I'm starving.'

Startled by his unexpected voice, Rose ran screaming from the room.

The doctor checked Angus's pulse. 'What can you remember, Mr McLoud?'

Angus winked at Rose. 'I was in a karaoke bar that didn't play any 70s music.' He began to sing. '*At first I was afraid, I was petrified...*'

The doctor shone a torch in Angus's eyes. 'Is he always this daft?'

'Always,' said Rose, glad to have her mad professor back.

The doctor added notes to his clipboard.

'OK, Doc, out with it; how long have I got?'

'It's difficult to say, but, if you stay out of fights, maybe another 30 years?'

'It wasn't dementia,' explained Rose; 'you have an underactive thyroid. The symptoms for the two conditions are similar: lack of concentration, short-term memory loss. It was an easy mistake...'

'Doctor, who is this strange woman, where is my wife, and where are my two lieutenants?'

'Can they come and visit him this afternoon, Doctor?' asked Rose.

'Not today; we need to run some tests and right now, Mr McLoud needs complete rest. But tomorrow afternoon should be fine.'

Rose sat by his bedside. 'They caught your attacker, by the way; he...'

'...drove a BMW and had red hair?'

'How did you...'

'Did I ever tell you, Rose? I went out with a redhead once. No hair, just a red head.'

Once alone, Angus beckoned a young nurse towards him and slipped a note into her hand. 'Nurse, could you please buy me a pair of these?'

She read the note. 'Mr McLoud. Really! At your age?'

The following day, the twins walked hesitantly towards the hospital bed on which a sleeping Angus lay. As they inched closer to the bed, he opened his eyes wide.

'Gotcha!'

They squealed with delight, jumped onto his bed and hugged him tightly.

'Stop that,' ordered Angus. 'You can't jump on beds in a hospital. Rose, fetch the handcuffs.'

'Don't be daft, Grandad,' they shouted. 'You haven't got any handcuffs.'

'Oh no?' he said, reaching under his pillow. 'Then what are these?'

+++++

Away in a Manger

No crib for his bed, the little lord Jesus laid down his sweet head. Beside him were his proud parents Mary and Joseph, the inn-keeper, and three wise men bearing gifts.

Outside, a bright light shone down from the starry sky above, illuminating the joyous celebration. Trumpets blew and angelic voices sang, as a man in a suit and tie appeared out of the shadows carrying a clipboard. He rapped his knuckles loudly on the stable door.

Those inside checked their scripts and scratched their heads. Who could it be? The inn-keeper opened the door. 'Who are you?'

'I'm from Bethlehem Council. We've received complaints about loud music, loud singing and bright lights. Do you have an entertainment licence?'

'You don't understand,' said Joseph, 'this is a celebration, a great occasion. The king is born today.'

'That's as may be, but European Union legislation clearly shows: no bright lights are permissible after 10pm. Who is responsible for the bright light above?'

'The baby,' explained Joseph, 'he's the son of...'

'Oh, that's right, blame the baby. I've heard it all now,' said the man from Bethlehem Council. 'I've also received complaints about someone riding a donkey without a crash-helmet, contrary to section 534, sub-section 2 of the Safe Highways Act. I suppose that was the baby as well.'

'Technically, yes,' explained Mary. 'I was pregnant with child, and rode on the donkey for four days.'

'For four days? I'll have to report you to the RSPCA. Donkeys have rights, you know. And for riding without a helmet, the spot fine is 60 shekels.'

'You can't fine Mary!' said a man holding a gift.

'And who are you to tell me what I can and can't do?'

'I'm one of the three wise men.'

'And who decided that you were wise? Have you won, *Who Wants to Win a Million Shekels*? Have you beaten the *Eggheads*?' And what are you holding?'

'A gift of gold for baby Jesus.'

'Gold? And where did it come from? To comply with the Bethlehem Financial Services Authority, can you show bank statements and proof of identity to satisfy money-laundering requirements?'

'No, of course not.'

'Well, I'm sorry, but I have no alternative but to confiscate it. You will have 48 hours to produce your paperwork at the council offices.'

The first wise man began to cry. 'But I've carried that gold for three days to give to the king of kings.'

'Don't be upset,' said the second wise man. 'We'll give the king the gift of frankincense between us.'

'Providing, of course, I can see a certificate that the product has not been tested on animals.'

'It's an aromatic herb obtained from trees, and specifically designed for personal use.'

'A herb for personal use, you say? Sounds like a Class B drug to me. I'll have to confiscate it.'

'But it is written...'

'It is also written in the European Union Book of Ethical Perfume Production,' said the council official, 'that no perfumes shall be tested on animals.'

'We'll give the gift of myrrh from all three of us,' said the third wise man, handing it over for inspection.

'Myrrh?' said the official, 'what's that, Egyptian Scrabble?'

'It is an essential oil, and the label clearly shows it has not been tested on animals.'

'Let me see.' The three wise men crossed their fingers. 'I'm sorry, but this container does not have a child-proof lock. I'll have to confiscate this also.'

The three wise men were stunned into silence, but the inn-keeper received some divine inspiration.

'Didn't I see you across town yesterday, issuing a spot fine to a shepherd?'

'That's right, Landlord. His animals were clearly obstructing Bethlehem High Street, contrary to the Animals and Countryside Act, sub-section 36.'

'Perhaps I could see *your* paperwork?'

'Certainly, Landlord. As you can see, I'm fully authorised by Bethlehem Central District.'

'In that case,' said the landlord, 'you have no authority here. My inn is situated in Bethlehem South District, so unless you want to be arrested for taking goods under false pretences, I suggest you clear off!'

Surprisingly, this encounter was omitted from the gospels of Matthew, Mark, Luke and John, and so, the nativity as we know it, came to pass.

Barbecue

'If he trespasses on my land again, I'll kill him.'

'Oh Barney, reel in that temper o' yours will ya? No wonder we got no friends.'

'Well, these strangers, they move into the valley and before you know it, they're taking over. And I 'eard they was vegetarians.'

'What we need is a barbecue, a get-to-know-your-neighbours party. You still got some home-brew left?'

'Well, yes, but...'

'Don't you "but" me, Barney, we got some food or not?'

'Still got that rack of ribs, but it will only feed around 30 I reckon.'

'Ribs it is, then.' Her loud voice echoed around their home. 'Junior, get yourself out here now!'

Barney junior stuck his head into the room. 'What?'

'Don't you "what" me, or I'll crack your skull. We're expecting visitors, so get tidying.'

'Go easy on him, Betty...'

'Go easy? I'll crack your skull an' all if you don't get movin', you great lump.'

As Betty swept, the dust rose into the air before settling back into the same place. Betty scratched her head, avoiding her new lump. They didn't have much, but all the same, that was no reason for untidiness. 'And clear away them weapons, Barney, we don't want no accidents.'

As Barney cleared up his mess, he felt a tug on his skin. 'Dad, come and see my drawings on the wall.'

'Never mind drawing on the wall, get yer room tidy or we're both for it.'

Later that day, the new people from down the valley, and close neighbours, began arriving for the big caveman party, many dressed in animal skins of all kinds; some even carried clubs, and as the home-made booze began to flow, men compared the size of their weapons and discussed hunting techniques.

Many children stared in wonder at Barney junior's drawings on the stone wall in his room.

The women drank fermented coconut wine and discussed family matters.

'Betty, that's a fine lump on your head, is Barney beating you again?'

'Oh yes, he's clubbing me nice and regular.'

Black smoke from the barbecue billowed high into the clear blue sky above the caveman party, and could be seen for miles around, attracting the attention of two scavengers on the look out for a free feed.

With a loud swish of their 40-foot wings, two pterodactyls swooped down into the plume of smoke and in the panic that ensued, carried away some brontosaurus ribs.

+++++

Working Out

Determined to enjoy a kiss and cuddle before Jack returned to the oil rig, Lizzie crept upstairs with two mugs of tea and placed them by the bed. Jack was still snoring loudly.

'Wakey wakey, rise and shine,' she shouted leaping back into bed, and before Jack realised what was happening, he had rolled into her waiting arms. After a quick cuddle (far too quick for Lizzie's liking), he sat up in bed and supped his tea, ending any opportunity for the passion she craved.

She slid dejectedly from the bed and removed her nightdress. She sensed the disapproval in his eyes and dressed hurriedly. No matter what she tried, he just didn't seem to fancy her anymore.

At breakfast as she stirred her bowl of sugar-free muesli, she watched Jack tuck into the sausage, bacon, eggs and fried bread that she had lovingly cooked for him. The seductive scent of the bacon teased her taste buds and just as she contemplated stealing the last piece of bacon off his plate, he stabbed it with his fork and shovelled it sideways into his mouth. She watched him chewing *her* piece of bacon and wondered if he was telepathic.

As he mopped up the egg juice with a slice of bread, Jack broke the silence.

'You're quiet this morning, pet, what's up?'

She wondered how to tell him that she missed his attention, and yet she knew the problem and it weighed heavily on her mind. In just 12 months of marriage, her weight had changed by almost 30 pounds.

'You had some bounce until your weight changed.'

Definitely telepathic, she thought. 'Guess I've been eating the wrong food.'

They both heard the air-brakes as the works coach hissed to a halt outside. Jack stood up from the table and reached for his coat. Lizzie moved forward in a last desperate attempt for a kiss and cuddle and received a peck on the cheek for her efforts.

'Do us both a favour,' he said, picking up his bag. 'Get your weight sorted out, will you? When we first met, you were bouncing with health and I loved you for it, but now your bounce has gone. You need to get back into shape, pet. Not for me, do it for you. You'll be happier in yourself - and you'll look better for it.'

She knew he was right. She had been in denial about her weight – until now.

'OK, Jack,' she said. 'I'll try working out, but no promises, mind.'

Jack's face lit up like a Christmas tree. 'Will you really try, pet? You just need to eat the right food and count the calories. It would be great to come home to the woman I fell in love with.' It was as if he could already see her as she used to be. With a sparkle in his eyes, he dropped his bag, moved quickly forward and planted a passionate kiss onto her lips. She was so surprised, she missed the opportunity to respond.

A horn sounded outside.

'I've got to go, love, the men are waiting, but I'll be back from the rig in 42 days' time. I'll count the days if you promise to count the calories.'

'It's a deal.' She leaned forward for another kiss, but he was already moving towards the door. As Jack closed the garden gate, he glanced at the front window, but Lizzie was nowhere in sight. She had already begun making plans. She had 42 days to regain her figure. It was going to take some doing, but her marriage and indeed her happiness, were on the line.

On the coach back to the oil rig, back to the job he loved because it kept him in good shape, Jack blamed himself for Lizzie's weight. It was only natural that she would get bored in his absence. Perhaps he should find another job? Then his thoughts turned to Lizzie and her promise to work out, and a smile spread across his face.

Lizzie's first stop was the library. One hour later she emerged with books on motivation, calorie control and exercise. Next stop was the supermarket where she scrutinised every label of every item before placing them into her trolley. At the checkout, her mind was a confusion of calories, proteins, carbohydrates, dietary fibres and emulsifiers. Calorie counting at the supermarket almost made her late for her afternoon job.

As she typed merrily away, Lizzie's new found zest for life was not lost on her work colleagues who teased her unmercifully.

'Give Jack a good sending off this morning, then?'
'Did the earth move?' asked another.

As soon as she arrived home from work, Lizzie made a cup of tea, grabbed half-a-dozen chocolate biscuits, and began reading the book on motivation. Rule one: picture your goal. She found the enlarged photo of her wedding, stuffed out of sight in the sideboard, and fixed it to the fridge, then went upstairs to the spare bedroom and pulled her rowing machine into the middle of the room, so that she could open the wardrobe doors.

She removed her wedding dress from the hanger, held it to her body, and longed to fit into it again, then she loaded her arms with her favourite outfits and hung them around the house, constant reminders of her goal. This was thirsty work. She boiled the kettle, made a cup of tea, and ate another handful of chocolate biscuits.

Placing the empty biscuit wrapper in the bin, she read about the delicate balance between calorie intake and exercise. Thirty pounds in six weeks was a near impossible target but, as the book explained, you have to push yourself. She broke the target down into weekly amounts. Five pounds a week, that's all it came down to: five pounds a week.

After making another cup of tea, she opened a packet of custard creams whilst reading about different exercises, many of which she had already used down at the gym to break up the lonely days during Jack's absence. Now she studied them more closely, learning which exercises burned off the most calories, and which burned off the least. She made another cup of tea and finished off the custard creams. Happy with her day's research, Lizzie enjoyed a cheese and mayonnaise sandwich, drank two glasses of red wine and sank into bed. Tomorrow, the hard work would begin.

The only interruptions during Lizzie's first two weeks of working out were phone calls from friends wondering where she was, but she quickly explained. 'I promised Jack that I would work out, and that's what

I'm doing. No, not at the gym, I'm working out at home. No, I don't need any help, thanks, but please, will you pray for me and Jack. We're having a few problems.'

At the end of two weeks, Lizzie finished a fried bacon and egg sandwich before going upstairs for the moment of truth. She stepped confidently onto the bathroom scales, and quickly jumped off again in horror. She trudged downstairs to place the scales on the laminate floor, hoping that the hard surface would influence the result. It didn't. She was way behind her target.

She flopped onto the sofa and had a good cry, before giving herself a talking to. Come on, it's only five pounds per week for six weeks. You saw the glint in his eyes before he left. She made a cup of tea, dunked a few chocolate biscuits and longed for the good old days. She needed more than prayers. She would not succeed on will-power alone. She picked up the phone.

During the next four weeks, Lizzie received plenty of encouragement from Roger, a long-term friend and her newly installed trainer. 'Come on, another one. Surely you can manage another one? Think of the look in Jack's eyes when he returns home.'

When Lizzie started to sag, Roger waved the wedding dress in front of her face. 'Do you want to fit in this dress again? Do you? Come on then, keep working out. You can manage another three at least.'

Lizzie did indeed manage another three, and as she counted the calories and counted the days, she felt her old confidence flowing back, especially when she caught Roger ogling the curves of her returning figure.

After six weeks, she stopped working out and stepped on the scales. She felt alive; the old confident Lizzie was back. She led Roger to the foot of the stairs and kissed him on the cheek. 'How can I ever thank you?' He looked at her like a lovesick puppy.

She kissed him again, she was so excited. 'Jack will be home soon,' she said, opening the front door. 'Thanks for all your help.'

After returning all of her favourite outfits to the wardrobe, she slipped into her old wedding dress. It was tight in places and she had tried in vain to hide the smell of mothballs with a liberal helping of Chanel No. 5, but if Jack looked at her the way he used to, then all of her hard work would be worth it.

Waiting in the hallway for Jack's return, Lizzie looked at her watch for the umpteenth time. Jack would be home any minute.

She heard the air-brakes as the coach hissed to a halt outside. Excitement spread through her body like an intravenous drug. She listened as his footsteps approached the front door; this was the moment of truth. She swallowed hard as his key turned in the lock and her heart skipped a beat as adrenalin completed two laps of honour around her blood vessels.

Jack pushed open the door and stared open-mouthed at the vision before him. He dropped his bag, rubbed his eyes, blinked twice and looked again.

Lizzie could wait no longer, so she gave him a twirl. 'Well, say something – how do I look?'

A broad grin spread across his face. 'You look absolutely fabulous, pet. I can't believe it. I never thought you'd work out that much.'

Lizzie explained. 'The first thing I did was stop going down the gym. Then I doubled up all of my calories and I began seriously working out at home. Look at my new curves.' To emphasise her point, she did another twirl. 'I've gained 30 pounds in six weeks!'

'Now that's what I call working out,' said Jack, shutting the front door behind him. He threw off his coat and moved towards her. 'Well, now that you look like a real woman and not a stick insect, give us a kiss you gorgeous lump.'

'Hang on a moment, hold it right there,' said Lizzie, keeping him at arm's length. Now's the time girl, go on, you can do it. It's now or never. 'Not so fast, Jack. I've been thinking. I need a man who loves me unconditionally, whatever shape I am – and right now, I'm not sure that's you.'

Nine months later after a quick divorce and a whirlwind romance, Lizzie walked down the aisle with Roger, her new adoring husband who loved her unconditionally. After only eight months of her second marriage, Lizzie's weight had again changed by almost 30 pounds, and Roger was delighted.

'Lizzie, did I forget to mention that triplets run in my family?'

+++++

Teacher's Pet

Miss Smart, a former student teacher, is our new athletics coach. She has deep blue eyes and, as you can imagine, is very fit. My hormones love her.

Last Thursday I ran faster than a geek at the launch of a new i-Phone, finishing the cross-country race well before the others. I head for the school changing rooms where, just as I had hoped, I bump into her. Not so much bump as collide, grab, to hold on to, so as not to fall down. So I am making seemingly innocent contact with her flesh, whilst at the same time wishing that I did not have so many spots on my face.

Then she gives me this look. Is this a moment, like? I want to bare my soul and tell her how I feel, but I bottle it and what comes out is, 'Oh my gosh, sorry miss, I wasn't looking where I was going.'

Then I realise that she is also holding me, but not because she is falling down, the light touch of her hand on my back sending shivers down my spine. I turn to walk away, totally freaked, scared and embarrassed, but she grabs my arm and turns me around, her grip sending adrenalin coursing through my 14-year-old body, and I freeze.

She whispers, 'I'm not sorry, Brad,' then she smiles, lets go of me and walks away, looking like, I don't know, strange. Interested maybe?

Does this mean something?

Like I would know.

Food, Glorious Food

(to be read in a Brummie accent)

At birth, I suckled
me mother's breast,
And from that day since,
I've been obsessed

With food and drink,
I just can't get enough,
Mum said I ate like a pig
at a trough.

As a schoolboy, Mars bars
satisfied me hunger,
Until as a teenager,
I tasted chips and beefburger.

Then I discovered the joy
caused by pints of Guinness,
And in me leather jacket,
I did look the business.

In me twenties I loved pies,
kebabs or fish in batter,
As long as it was greasy
it didn't really matter.

Unless I started the day with
a full English brekkie,
I had this empty feeling
inside of me belly.

In me thirties, I didn't care
about animals and slaughtering,
A T-bone steak or chops
soon got me mouth a-watering.

But one thing I couldn't stand,
try as I might.
That's right, you've guessed it,
the taste of Marmite.

In me forties me taste buds
went completely wild.
I ate all types of curry,
hot, spicy and mild.

My breath was rank –
but what the hell!
Foreign food had me under
its hypnotic spell.

In me fifties I developed
a middle aged spread.
'You must start to eat less,'
my doctor said.

I'd become an overweight
couch potato,
Owner of an un-healthy
height-to-weight ratio.

In me sixties I tried rabbit food
and low-fat yoghurts.
But all they did was give me
a dose of the trots.

Me brain and me senses
are still perfectly sound.
And me wheelchair is comfy,
I can still get around.

Should I blame me mother
for breastfeeding me?
Or sue McDonalds, the chippy,
or Cadburys?

I doubt I'll reach seventy now,
not even sixty-seven.
So please pray that there are
cheeseburgers up in heaven.

+++++

'I Demand to See the Captain!'

'We demand another room!'

'This way, keep moving please, move right down the corridor, that's right, any room you like, and there's plenty of room on the top deck.'

'Excuse me, I'm talking to you.'

'Can't you see I'm busy? Can't it wait? – keep moving please,' said the harassed helper.

'I don't like your tone. I demand to speak to the captain of this vessel.'

'He's as busy as I am. We didn't expect them all at once – down to the left or right, that's it, keep moving, there are plenty of rooms.'

'I hope they get a better room than ours.'

'And what exactly is *wrong* with your room?

'Our neighbours on one side smell disgusting, and those on the other side keep tapping the wall.'

'I'll see if I can find the captain. Your names are?'

'Mr and Mrs Partridge.'

Ten minutes later, the harassed helper returned. 'I've had a word with the captain on your behalf, Mr and Mrs Partridge; and he said, "Your neighbours are skunks and woodpeckers, and if you don't like it," and Noah really stressed this last point, "you can always leave the ark".'

The Great Escape

Charles, Sid and Doris sat silently in front of the bay window in the lounge of the Utopia Retirement Home, looking out at the wheelie bins and recycling containers. Charles, the eldest by more than two decades, brushed imaginary hairs off his suit. 'The sun will be round in a minute.'

'What shape is it usually, then?' asked Sid.

Doris stared at the empty birdcage. 'What happened to Joey?'

Charles adjusted his cravat. 'He probably died of boredom.'

'Yesterday, he was as happy as Larry,' chirped Sid.

Doris yawned. 'Where is Larry, anyway?'

'Larry's been gone a while – to Pilates, I think.'

'Oh dear. I didn't realise they were deadly. I put cream on mine.'

'Doris, I said "Pilates", not piles. It's a programme designed to stretch you, you know, like *Loose Women*.'

'Ooh, I like *Loose Women*.'

'I'm also partial to loose women,' said Sid, 'and you're wrong Charles. Larry went off to Zumba.'

Doris frowned. 'Why's he gone to Africa?'

Charles looked to the heavens. 'Larry likes to keep busy. He's even joined that new meditation class. It's better than sitting around doing nothing, I suppose.'

Sid nodded towards the new nurse approaching with the drinks trolley. 'I don't trust her, this one with the funny name.'

'It's not a funny name; it's Elena Svetlanka,' explained Charles.

'From Poland?'

'No Sid, she's from Accrington Stanley.'

'Well, I still don't trust her. She gave me a Viagra tablet with my cocoa last night.'

'How can you be sure?' said Doris, glad for something exciting to talk about.

'Well, you know how I wake up stiff every morning...'

Charles interrupted before Sid could go into details. 'That's the trouble with you youngsters, always going on about sex. My Gertrude and I were never like that, apart from the odd time when she would tie me to the mangle and spank me with the coal shovel, but let's not speak ill of someone who's passed to the other side.'

'Is she dead?'

'Might as well be, Sid; she joined the Green Party.'

Nurse Elena handed out the drinks. 'How are the three musketeers this morning?'

Charles answered for the group. 'We're all fine, and looking forward to another action-packed day.'

'That's good to hear; now Charles, can I ask you a question?'

Charles puffed up his chest and adjusted his cravat. She obviously knew intelligence when she saw it. 'What would you like to know, my dear?'

'Why do you have shampoo in your bathroom when you're bald?'

Charles jumped to his feet, his toupee almost sliding off his head. 'I still have my pride, goddammit!'

'Calm down,' shouted Sid, 'keep your hair on.'

Nurse Elena grinned wickedly, before moving on with the tea trolley.

'May I suggest we double check any tablets *she* dispenses?' said Charles. 'We must make sure we don't take a laxative and a sleeping pill at the same time. We must be on our guard. We're deep in enema territory.'

Doris spat out her tea. 'Nurse Elena knows I'm diabetic, but she still keeps putting sugar in my tea. I think she's in league with my daughter who's trying to kill me off for a share of my inheritance just because I wouldn't buy her a pony when she was ten.'

Back in his chair, Charles adjusted his toupee. 'Maybe it's incompetence, Doris?'

'Oh no, I'm quite solid, thank you.'

'I said "incompetence" – oh, it doesn't matter.'

Sid tried to lighten the atmosphere. 'When I was young, I used to take acid and climb trees, now I take antacid and climb the walls. I've had enough of this place. I know, let's escape and burn the midnight oil until 10 o'clock.'

'Count me in,' said Doris. 'Let's go on a spending spree. That'll teach my daughter for putting me in this hell-hole to rot away. What goes around comes around. What do they call it – korma?'

'I think you mean karma,' corrected Sid, 'but we could have a curry first, followed by a few drinks. It would be nice to swop the smell of urine for the smell of Woodbine, beer and a vindaloo.'

'And just how do you plan to get through security?'

'That's where you come in, Charlie. Are you going to stay behind and let Nurse Elena finish you off, or do you want to join the great escape?'

Nurse Elena smirked at them through the window whilst having a crafty smoke by the wheelie bins.

'OK Sid, count me in. We'll hold our first escape meeting at 3pm after the quiz.'

Question eight: name five African animals.

Sid quickly answered, 'That's easy, four elephants and a tiger.' Charles ignored him and wrote down *elephant, tiger, lion, zebra* and *monkey.*

Question nine: name a long-necked bird.

Sid suggested Naomi Campbell, Doris suggested a stork, and Charles wrote down *emu.*

Question ten: Name the two Gentlemen of Verona.'

'I know this, I know this,' said Sid. 'It's Butch Cassidy and...'

His patience starting to wear thin, Charles looked down his nose at Sid. 'It's Valentine and Proteus.'

'Are you always right, Charles?' asked Sid.

'94% of the time, yes, so why should I worry about the other 10%?'

As Nurse Elena gathered up the answer papers, Sid responded to the look Charles gave him. 'I'm not really daft, Charles. I once read a play by Shakespeare.'

'Did you now, and which one was it?'

'William, of course.'

Doris laughed so much, she wet herself.

After the quiz, Charles chaired the escape committee. 'There's no point in trying to escape through the back yard; there are too many steps. The best way is through the front door, but how do we get our hands on a front door key?'

'I know you're gonna find this hard to believe,' said Sid, 'but many years ago, when God was a boy, I was a magician's assistant.'

Charles scratched his toupee, causing it to wriggle across his head like a moving caterpillar. 'And that's relevant to our escape plans because...?'

'Magic is all sleight of hand,' explained Sid, showing a bunch of keys. 'I lifted these from Nurse Elena's pocket during the quiz.'

'Great work, Sid, that gets us through the front door. What we need now is a diversion so that we can slip out unnoticed; any suggestions?'

Doris raised her right hand.

'There's no need to be formal, dear, just say what you think.'

'Let's push that new lady Beryl Perkins down the stairs.'

'That's hardly fair, Doris.'

'Fair? Is it fair that she talks all the way through *Loose Women*? She's asking for it if you want my opinion.'

'What about setting off the fire alarm?'

'That's no good, Sid; everyone will evacuate outside just in time to point and shout, "Look, over there, the three musketeers are escaping".'

'I know,' said Charles, 'My room is on the second floor. If I leave my bathroom tap turned on and I leave my plug in the sink; after a while, water should come down through the ceiling. That should create a lengthy diversion, and let's face it, we're not exactly quick on our feet; we need all the time we can get. Let's go and pack a few things... hang on, here comes the nurse.'

Nurse Elena lifted Sid off the armchair and into his wheelchair. 'I take it the three musketeers are joining us for lunch? It's steak and ale pie followed by spotted dick.'

Doris released her brakes and grabbed the wheels of her wheelchair. 'I can't remember the last time I had spotted dick. Come on, Sid, I'll race you. Are you coming, Charles?'

'I'll catch up with you in a moment, please save me a seat.'

Doris led the way to the large dining room, closely followed by Nurse Elena, who pushed Sid.

'So what do you three talk about? You always look as if you're plotting something.'

'Imagination, nurse, is about all we have left.'

One hour later, as Doris finished her last spoonful of spotted dick; drips of water began to fall on the tablecloth.

+++++

Oh, to be 16 Once Again

Alone within the Magic Circle and beneath the waxing moon, the white witch transcended the physical world and took his mind to higher levels of consciousness. With hands outstretched, he drew a circle of protection around himself three times, visualising white light coming from his fingers.

These movements caused the four candles, green at the north point, red to the south, blue to the west and yellow to the east, to flicker, sending shadows dancing wildly across and around his 50-year-old naked torso. He visualised his goal, projecting it into the vast universe as he began reciting his opening mantra: *I have the power within me, spells are my birthright to perform. I have the power within me, spells are my birthright to perform.*

He chanted faster and faster creating a continuous vibration and when his mind was cleared of worldly thoughts and focussed entirely on his goal, he slowed his heart and his breathing and started a second chant: *I bow to the light within, I am one with god, I am a being of light and I rid my being of all negativity.*

His bones creaked as he knelt down to complete the preparations that would guarantee success. He lit the solitary black candle inside the circle and added the required ingredients to the chalice of water. First, two spoonfuls of Vermain, then one spoonful of salt, mixed thoroughly with a piece of petrified wood. He passed a rock seven times through the candle flame as he poured out his heart's desire: *Candle, herb, rock, water and salt, to the elements of the universe, I exalt. Oh to be 16 once again, and to have a body free from pain.* Nine times he chanted this and with each chant he touched the rock against various parts of his body.

With the spell completed, he replaced his robe and gathered together his magical accessories.

As he returned through the woods to his basement flat, the early morning silence was disturbed by the hoot of an owl, and clouds drifted across the waxing moon.

Once inside his flat, Lucien opened his Book of Shadows to record the details of his latest spell. Everything had worked perfectly; a younger body was guaranteed. As he drifted off to sleep, he could feel his body starting to change.

On waking, Lucien felt completely different. He leapt out of bed, free from pain at last. On youthful legs, his chest covered by a *New Kids on the Block* T-shirt, he bounded into the bathroom to check his mirror image, only to recoil in horror. He looked again at his reflection, and his new 16-year-old hands traced the lumps and bumps of a face full of angry red zits, and as he opened his mouth to scream, light bounced off the metal brace clamped to his teeth.

Editor's Note: *To safeguard impressionable readers from trying to re-create this spell for eternal youth, I lied when I said:* Nine times he chanted, *oh to be 16 once again, and to have a body free from pain.* You only need to chant this seven times.

A Very Special Gift

Galilee must be the most boring place on earth, thought Mary, as she washed clothes in the back room; nothing exciting ever happened. Then a melodic voice called out at the front of the house.

'Hello, Mary? Are you home?'

Mary dried her hands and appeared by the doorway. 'And who wants to know?' She looked at the strange figure dressed in white robes.

'I am the angel Gabriel, do not be afraid.'

She gave him a puzzled look. 'You don't scare me, sunshine.' She turned him around slightly. 'Are those wings for real?'

'Yes they are, Mary, and I bring you unbelievable news.'

'Have I won the Judean Lottery?'

'Mary, it's even better than that; you have been chosen for a very special gift.'

Mary shook her head. 'Not another one. Can't you see the sticker on the door? No doorstep traders. Clear off.'

'But I have a message from the Lord God on high; you are to have a baby.'

'Pull the other one, it's got bells on. Go on, sling your hook.'

'Don't shoot me, I'm only the messenger. You have

been chosen to have a special baby.'

'Don't tell me, let me guess; you're the one chosen and it's fallen on your shoulders to make me pregnant. Do you think I'm stupid?'

'Good heavens no, I'm not the chosen one; my task is simply to deliver the message.'

'Well, I'm not interested, so scram.'

'Wait, I have to deliver the rest of the message: You will be made pregnant by the Holy Spirit...'

'What? No cuddles behind the synagogue? No whispers of sweet nothings in my ear? Not even a goblet of Chateau Babylon?'

'...and your baby boy shall be called Jesus.'

'Listen, Gabriel, before you fly back to where you came from, let me make myself perfectly clear: *if* I decide to lose my virginity, and *if* I give birth to a baby boy, it will be named after my boyfriend, Eric.'

'Eric? Isn't your boyfriend Joseph the carpenter?'

'No, it's Eric, and he's a tax collector.'

The angel scratched his wings. 'Is this 42 Damascus Drive?'

'No, this is number 32. You want Mary and Joseph; they live at number 42, five doors down, on the left.'

'Oh, I'm sorry,' said the angel Gabriel, 'these SatNavs are blooming useless.'

+++++

(Based on an idea by Richard Stableford)

41

Do You Fancy a Bite?

Megan squinted through the rain-battered window. He was late. Maybe his wife had made plans he couldn't get out of, again? Maybe he was stuck in traffic? Her questions were answered by a text message. He promised me the earth, and now he's dumped me by text. Megan was fuming. She threw on her raincoat and hit the street, teardrops mingling with the rainfall. She longed for true romance with a tall, dark, handsome man by moonlight. Was that too much to ask?

She rushed around the corner, mobile phone in hand, and collided with a tall figure rushing in the opposite direction. Her phone slipped from her grasp, bounced once, and disappeared down a drain. She sank to her knees, frantically clawing at the drain.

Strong hands lifted her easily and pulled her into the shelter of a betting-shop doorway. 'Stay here, there's no point in us both getting wet. I'll get your phone.'

What are the odds that's he's another lowlife, she thought, as she watched him try to lift the drain cover to reach her phone, and what kind of man wears a cape these days?

He returned empty-handed, shrugging powerful shoulders, his six-foot frame dwarfing her small stature. 'I can bring some tools and try to retrieve it for you tomorrow.'

Megan looked up into the most hypnotic blue eyes

she'd ever seen.

'Look, I know we've got off on the wrong foot, but there's a steakhouse across the road and I'm starving. The least that I can do is treat you to a meal. Do you fancy a bite?'

He was tall, dark and handsome, and she was hungry. What was the worst that could happen? Despite the fact he was a total stranger, she could really do with some company right now. 'Sure, why not?'

Inside the steakhouse, he led her to a table in a dimly-lit corner and helped remove her coat. Masterful *and* considerate; maybe he's not a lowlife after all. 'Thank you, Lord,' she whispered.

He offered his hand. 'My name's Jake.'

'My name's Megan.' She placed her small delicate hand into his powerful fingers, hoping her knight in shining armour would lift it to his lips. Knight in shining armour? Calm down girl. He gave a perfunctory handshake, the kind you would give an unwanted relative at Christmas.

His deep voice brought her back to reality. 'Megan, what would you like to drink?'

She was cold, soaked to the skin, phoneless and feeling sorry for herself. There was only one cure. 'A brandy, if that's OK.'

'Good idea. Waiter, two brandies please.'

'So, tell me Jake, are you single, or married?'

'Divorced, so if you're looking for a husband, count me out. Once bitten...'

She began to relax; he was laid back *and* good looking, except for a very pale complexion, but why on earth was he wearing such a strange outfit?

'Penny for your thoughts?'

'Did you get dressed in the dark, or are you wearing those clothes for a bet?'

Jake feigned upset. 'I'll have you know, this purple shirt and red tie combination is my favourite outfit, and they go brilliantly with my cape, don't you think?'

'No wonder you're divorced.'

They looked at menus. 'So, Jake, will your credit card stretch to starters?'

'It will, but I can't see anything I want to sink my teeth into, except you.'

Megan blushed.

The waiter placed two brandies on the table. 'Are you ready to order?'

'Yes,' began Jake, 'I'd like my steak rare because I like to see blood oozing out as I cut it.'

'And would you like a side dish? Garlic bread, perhaps?'

'Certainly not! Don't bring garlic anywhere near me, or I'll break out in a rash.'

'And would you like another drink, sir?'

'Yes, I'll have a Bloody Mary.'

Megan's heart skipped several beats. Pale skin – hates garlic – wears a cape - loves blood? Calm down girl; remember what Bart Simpson said: vampires are make-believe, just like elves, gremlins and Eskimos.

'And madam? How would you like your steak?'

'Wooden – I mean, I wouldn't want it rare. Can I have it well-d-d-done?'

'And would you like a side dish?'

'Yes, garlic sauce, and make it a double helping.'

'I'll see what I can do, madam; and to drink?'

'Another brandy please, and make it a large one!'

Jake seemed amused by her discomfort.

In an effort to calm her nerves, Megan began asking questions. 'Were you born around here?'

'No, I was born in L.A.'

Megan sipped her brandy: thank God it wasn't Transylvania. 'Los Angeles?'

'No, Long Ashton near Bristol; but my family originate from Transylvania.' He studied her face.

Megan felt uncomfortable. 'If I didn't know better, I'd think you were a hungry vampire out on the prowl.'

Jake sipped his brandy, showing no reaction to her statement.

The waiter returned with their drinks and told them food would be another 15 minutes. Megan drank more brandy before rising shakily to her feet. 'That gives me time to freshen up; I won't be long.'

She hurried into the ladies' restroom, entered a cubicle and bolted the door. He was a stranger who acted strangely, talked strangely, and dressed strangely. What was she thinking? Her instincts told her she was safe, but what if...? She decided to phone for back-up and reached into her bag. Damn; no phone.

The restroom door opened. She held her breath. She heard two or three footsteps, then silence, except for a low click, click, click. Is he cracking his knuckles? If he's come for me, I won't become a blood donor without a fight. She grabbed the loo brush, quietly unlocked the cubicle door and jumped out waving the brush above her head, only to find a woman sending a text message. The woman froze in terror.

'Don't move. I think a vampire is after my blood and I need your help.'

'It's not my help that you need, love, it's counselling.'

'Do you want my blood on your hands? Well, do you? I thought not, so give me your phone.'

Fearful of being assaulted by a maniac wielding a toilet brush, the young woman obeyed.

Megan dialled 999. 'Hello – police – come quickly, it's urgent, I'm in grave danger – Where am I? - I'm in the Quick Bite Steakhouse – that's right – the one in Artery Road - a vampire wants me for his dessert.'

The young woman snatched back her phone. 'OK, you've had your fun, I've heard enough of this. You need help.'

Alone again, Megan checked the toilet windows; all were barred. She was trapped. She left the toilets to find the steakhouse almost empty. She considered bolting for the exit, but the table he had chosen was between her and the exit, and she knew that if she ran, he would easily catch her. She felt safer in the restaurant. At least there was a chef and a waiter and the police were on their way. She returned to her seat.

'I was just about to send out a search party.' As he laughed loudly, Jake gave her a first clear view of his teeth.

Oh – my – God! He's got fangs!

The waiter placed their food on the table. Megan immediately smothered her steak with garlic sauce and gulped down a mouthful. Stay calm, girl, eat plenty of garlic sauce, and keep him talking.

'So Jake, w-what do you do for a living?'

'I used to work at the blood bank.'

Megan didn't like the sound of that. 'Used to?'

'They sacked me for drinking on the job.'

Megan gulped down more garlic-covered steak. He was toying with her, like a lion with a wounded gazelle.

The waiter returned. 'Is everything OK with your meals?'

'More garlic sauce and another brandy,' spluttered Megan between mouthfuls. Come on, police, hurry.

Jake grinned at his victim. 'It's pretty obvious what you're thinking, so why don't you ask me?'

Megan swallowed more garlic-covered steak.

'You think I'm a vampire, don't you?'

She stuffed more steak into her mouth. 'Well, are you?'

Jake bared his fangs for a second time. 'Of course I am.'

Megan passed out.

Jake paid the bill, effortlessly scooped Megan into his powerful arms and carried her outside. As he turned down the canal towpath, the hooting of an owl mingled with the distant sound of police sirens. He found a bench, and gently laid her down.

Under the light of the full moon, Megan opened her eyes to find Jake crouching over her. She felt her neck for bite marks. 'Have you done it? Am I now a vampire?'

His blue eyes glinted in the moonlight. 'I'm sorry to disappoint you.'

She felt her neck a second time. 'But you said...'

'...that I was a vampire? Yes, but you fainted before I could finish.'

'But I saw your pointed teeth?'

He pulled rubber fangs from his pocket. 'Oh, these; I put them on while you were in the toilet.'

'You mean: it was all an act?'

'I *am* a vampire - at the Playhouse Theatre for the next three weeks, and I always try out my costume beforehand; it helps me to get into the role.'

Megan sat upright and punched his arm. 'I can't believe you let me eat all that garlic sauce. I was so scared, I even called the police.'

'Alas, dear Megan, I know them well. Methinks it was only last month; I played a transvestite hooker. Naturally, I had to try out the costume...'

This was not the moonlit romance Megan had been longing for, until Jake pulled her to her feet and kissed her on the lips.

'Megan, let's make a deal. If I promise to dress sensibly and you promise not to eat so much garlic sauce, why don't we meet at the steakhouse tomorrow night about 8pm? I'll bring your phone, and then, if you fancy a bite...'

+++++

Male Escort

'So tell me,' asked Kate, as Mike, her escort, opened the car door for her. 'Why are you still single?'

'Must be all the time I spend with married women. Where is your husband, anyway? Out on family business again? I hope he's looking after you.'

'If he was looking after me, I wouldn't need your services,' she teased.

'His loss is my gain,' replied Mike.

Kate studied his profile as they neared the club. Mike was by far her favourite escort. Unlike her husband, he had rugged good looks, he was the strong and silent type, he had a good sense of humour, and most important of all, he made her feel safe.

'Nearly there now,' said Mike. 'Have you brought a change of clothing?'

Kate's excitement was building now. 'You'll have to wait and see. Have you brought my protection?'

Mike smiled. 'Of course!'

They reached the club and Mike opened the car door to help her out.

'I'll meet you on the balcony in 20 minutes.'

Twenty minutes later, to a tremendous round of applause, Kate, the Duchess of Cambridge took her seat in the royal box under a burning sun, to watch the Wimbledon Men's Singles semi-finals. In the shadows stood Mike, her favourite bodyguard, armed with her protection; Amber Solaire, Factor 26.

Where There's a Will

'Mother dearest. I'm so glad we now have your paperwork in order, especially your Will. We don't want to leave a mess, now, do we? What was it you always used to say? Everything in its place, and a place for everything, and I've found the perfect place for you, mother dearest.

'Now, mother, let's do something with those eyelashes. Keep your head still now; I don't want to poke you in the eye.'

As requested, mother remained still, as her daughter carefully applied mascara.

Rose held up a mirror. 'There, mother, now doesn't that look better. What's the matter, cat got your tongue? Now, I want you to look your best for your new home, so let's do something with your complexion, it has really gone pasty.' She dabbed rouge on her mother's cheeks.

'There now, how does that look? You think you need a bit more rouge? You know what, I think you're right.' She lowered the mirror and applied more rouge. Even as a child, Rose had enjoyed putting make-up on her mother's face.

'Oh mother, look, I've got red all over my fingers. Stay where you are, please, I'll just go and wash my hands.'

Stepping over the fresh corpse of the will consultant, Rose moved from the living room into the kitchen, where she plunged her hands under the cold water tap, watching in fascination as tap-water created intricate red patterns and splashes in the white ceramic sink as it washed the blood and rouge from her hands, before disappearing down the plughole. She also washed the blood from the carving knife and replaced it in the cutlery drawer. Everything in its place, and a place for everything.

Rose put mother's signed Will in a safe place before helping mother into the passenger seat. 'It's time for me to take you to your new home now, and I know just how much you love vegetables, so I've chosen the ideal place. Just you wait 'til you see it. Let's turn the heater up a bit, there's a definite chill in the air.

'Here we are at last, mother. Now let's get you settled into your new home, and I promise, cross my heart and hope to die, that I will come and visit you with your favourite flowers, whenever I can spare the time.'

By torchlight, Rose buried her mother's severed head in an allotment.

+++++

Gold-Digger

'I don't understand why you're in such a hurry to get married; anyone would think that you had to.' Marcus tried to keep the annoyance out of his voice.

'Son, I know it's only been 12 months since your mother...'

'There, you've admitted it yourself. It's too soon. How long have you known this woman anyway?'

'I suggest you ease back on your temper; that's if you value your allowance and university fees.'

'I'm surprised you managed to find time to meet someone else. Your company always comes first. It's what drove mum...'

'It's not *my* company, it's *our* company. When you've qualified, there's a job waiting for you.'

Marcus chewed the inside of his cheek. The last thing on earth he wanted to do was work with his father.

'Anyway, that's the future, son; let's get back to the present. I expect you and Kirsty to be home this weekend to meet Sharon.'

His father was fat, thinning on top, drank too much and was married to his business, hardly husband material. This was wrong. She was obviously a gold-digger after his father's money.

'Son, are you still there?'

'Yes, I'm still here.'

'I'm on the way out to Germany to pitch for a contract, and we'll be back in England on Saturday.'

'We? Is *she* going with you?'

'*She* goes by the name of Sharon; we're engaged and getting married, of course she's coming with me. We'll be back to the house around 1900 hours. I've arranged for food to be delivered around 1930 hours and I expect you both to be there.'

Marcus slammed down the receiver. Yes sir, no sir, three bags full.

Sharon pressed a button on the side of her seat and watched it transform underneath her into a full-length bed. She pressed the button again; the motor groaned in protest at her weight as it pushed her back into the upright position. 'I think I could get used to flying Business Class.'

Joe was thinking over his sorry pitch for the contract. 'I'm sorry dear, what did you say?'

'It doesn't matter, love. Just try to get some sleep, and stop worrying. I can handle your children.'

'Kirsty will be no problem; Marcus will be the troublesome one.'

'Aren't you forgetting something?'

'What's that?'

'I'm good under interrogation.' She passed him a glass of champagne. 'Here's to a long and happy future together.' If only that could be true, thought Joe, as he drank the toast.

Dragging two suitcases through his front door, Joe paused for breath and then hugged his fiancée tightly. 'Welcome to your new home.'

'Wow, nice place, much bigger than my flat.'

'Yes, we have six bedrooms and four reception rooms, one of which is a photographic studio.'

'Who's the photographer?'

'Marcus. Between you and me, he's not very good, but it keeps him out of mischief. Marcus? Kirsty? Where are you?'

Marcus and Kirsty had been sharing a joint on the back porch when the front doorbell chimed. They casually strolled into the room, and as introductions were made, the doorbell chimed again.

'Good, that'll be the food,' said Joe, immediately delegating duties. 'Kirsty, show Sharon where the kitchen is and help her lay the table, oh, and fetch three bottles of wine from the cellar, the good stuff from the top shelf. Marcus, don't just stand there, answer the door before they take the food away, and bring the two pink suitcases in from the porch.' Clenching and unclenching his fists, Marcus resisted the urge to salute.

Although of slim build, Kirsty picked at her food. Marcus, like his father, had a healthy appetite and, between mouthfuls, studied Sharon closely. A typical gold-digger, he thought: middle-aged with dyed-blonde hair, big boobs and the ability to wrap men around her little finger. Her green eyes were alert but cold, like the eyes of an over-fed predator too lazy to pounce.

'So where did you guys meet?'

'You'll never guess, son. We met in a bank.'

Typical hunting ground for a gold-digger, thought Marcus. 'And how long ago was that?'

Sharon looked up from her plate of food and turned to Joe. 'I reckon it's been six months, what do you reckon, love?' As common as muck, decided Marcus, certainly not right for his father.

Joe rose to his feet. 'Please raise your glasses, kids, I have an announcement to make. We've set the date: we're getting married in three weeks time.'

The announcement drew mixed reactions. Kirsty offered immediate congratulations and asked excitedly if she could be a bridesmaid; Marcus considered slitting his wrists.

The wine and conversation flowed between Joe, Sharon and potential bridesmaid Kirsty, but there was only one thing on Marcus's mind. He had three weeks to get rid of this gold-digger.

Marcus stood up from the table. 'Please excuse me, folks, I fear I've eaten far too much. I'll say goodnight and see you all in the morning.'

'On your way upstairs, son, can you take Sharon's pink suitcases and put them outside the master bedroom?'

Once inside his bedroom, Marcus grabbed his laptop. Who was this woman, trying to drag his father down the aisle? Although it was a long-shot, he Googled the name from the suitcase labels, *Sharon McIntyre*. It didn't take long to find her. Not only was she a gold-digger, she was a gold-digger of the worst kind. Satisfied with his research, he collapsed into bed and drifted off to sleep.

Tired from the flight, Joe was the second person to make excuses and retire to bed.

Sharon poured out two more glasses of wine. 'I'll be up soon, love; we'll just finish off this bottle.' Then she turned to Kirsty. 'So, how's Marcus doing at university?'

'Well,' giggled Kirsty...

The following morning, Sharon was the first to rise. She found mugs and coffee in the kitchen and, cradling her first cup of the day, looked admiringly out of the window at the large manicured garden and ornamental ponds. She opened a window and listened to the dawn chorus.

'Nice view, isn't it?' said Marcus, deliberately making her jump. 'Enjoy it while you can, because you won't be here much longer.'

'Who got out the wrong side of their cage this morning?'

'I did, and my cage has a computer, and it's so difficult to hide a murky past, especially one as murky as yours.' He poured himself a black coffee.

'Who's a clever boy then? I bet you even changed your own nappy when you were a baby. So, what did you find?'

'Enough to get rid of you, that's for sure, and please pull your robe together. Your assets may have hypnotised my father, but they won't work on me.'

Ignoring his request, Sharon gave the kind of sensuous grin that suggested anonymous sex in a back alley. 'So, I assume that you found out about husband number one, the car accident?'

'And husband number two.'

'Oh yes, the heart attack. Is that all?'

'You mean there's more?' Marcus couldn't understand why she remained so calm.

'Just one more; something to do with his liver, the coroner said. You're not as good as your father, he found out about all three.'

Marcus choked on his coffee. 'What do you mean?'

'Your father knows all about my unfortunate past, there are no secrets between us. He's also told me about his first wife and how she left...'

'She didn't leave, he drove her out...'

'My, you are carrying around emotional baggage. Would you like the phone number of a good shrink?'

'With your assets,' he said, deliberately staring into his coffee, 'a gold-digger like you could trap any man you want, so why are you chasing my father?'

'If you must know, he's the one doing the chasing.'

'And you expect me to believe that?'

'Why don't you ask him? And don't forget to tell him that you've been a naughty boy. Fancy dropping out of university three months ago and pocketing the fees; he will be disappointed.'

'How did you...'

'Kirsty, bless her. Some people just can't keep secrets after a few drinks and a joint.'

Marcus was back to square one; Sharon had covered her back well. 'So why are you in a hurry to get him down the aisle?'

'He's the one in the hurry. Maybe it's true love? Have you ever been in love, Marcus? Ever been desired by someone?'

'This wedding has nothing to do with love. It's wrong and I won't let it happen.'

'Poor little Marcus, is some nasty woman taking your daddy away?'

'You can take my dad away with pleasure, but you'll not take my inheritance, you gold-digging bitch.'

'At last, you show your true colours. You disliked me before you even saw me. Sounds to me like you're the gold-digger.'

Marcus spun on his heel, and stormed off.

Later, on a bench in the garden, far away from the house, Mark and Kirsty shared another joint.

'She's killed three husbands already. She's clever, but she's not going to make Dad number four.'

Kirsty took another drag. 'Whatever you plan to do, I don't want to know.'

'That's fine by me. Just one thing, though: if I get caught sleepwalking...'

'But you haven't done that for ages.'

'...you say that you found me sleepwalking twice last month.'

'What you gonna do?'

'Get some photographs of Sharon in bed, and then try to blackmail her or something.'

'What if she wakes up?'

'I dunno, I'll say I was sleepwalking.'

'But how will you explain the camera?'

'I'll hide it.'

'Where, don't you sleepwalk in the nude?'

'I'll think of somewhere; the point is, if I get caught, you've seen me sleepwalking recently.'

The wedding drew near and Marcus was running out of time and ideas. Several times he'd crept into the master bedroom, only to find Sharon snuggled under the quilt.

It had been a glorious summer's day and like a couple of lovebirds, Joe and Sharon had spent the day lazing in the sun. In the evening, it was still humid as Marcus tip-toed into the master bedroom once again. Bingo! His father was snoring loudly and Sharon lay naked and only half-covered by the quilt. A gentle breeze from the open window caressed his thighs, making his skin prickle, as he adjusted his camera to allow photography in the semi-dark with no flash.

He carefully pulled the quilt to one side, exposing more of Sharon's naked body, and began taking pictures. A strong gush of wind blew through the window, ruffling the curtains. Sharon half-turned and reached out, almost touching his equipment with her fingers, before grabbing the quilt and pulling it back over her. Jumping back, Marcus almost dropping his camera. Holding his breath, he crept slowly and quietly back to the safety of his bedroom.

The following morning, Sharon eyed Marcus suspiciously. 'Has anyone seen my mobile phone? I'm sure it was on my bedside table last night.'

'Maybe you dropped it at the dress-fitters yesterday?' said Kirsty.

'That's possible, Kirsty, but unlikely.'

'Don't worry, it's bound to turn up,' said Marcus.

Sharon and Kirsty were out of the house for their final dress-fittings, and Joe sat on his veranda, happy and contented. Tomorrow, he would be married. Marcus joined him on the veranda.

'Dad, there's something you need to know.'

'If it's about Sharon's past, son, I know every detail about her three late husbands. We've talked through the circumstances and I can assure you, she is definitely the right woman for me.'

'It's not about the past, Dad, it's about last night.'

Excited voices filled the house as Sharon and Kirsty returned. Joe waited in the lounge, his face like thunder. 'Kirsty,' he barked, 'go to your room, and don't come down until I tell you.'

As soon as his daughter was out of the room, he let rip. 'Sharon, how could you, and with my own son? Pack your bags and get out.'

'But Joe, what am I supposed to have done?'

'You tried to seduce my son last night.'

'No I didn't, I swear it on the graves of my three dead husbands.'

'Well, how does he know about the heart tattoo on the inside of your left thigh?'

'I've no idea.'

Joe threw several large photos of her naked body onto the coffee table. She was speechless.

'I didn't believe him at first until we found this.' He threw her mobile phone onto the table.

'Where did you find it?'

'When Marcus told me you took photos of each other, I called him a liar, and he suggested that if we found your phone, it would confirm his story. So we searched the master bedroom and I found your conveniently lost mobile phone, hidden under the mattress on your side of the bed. How do you explain the photos on your phone, taken last night?'

Looking at the photographs on her phone, Sharon shook her head in confusion. 'But I would never do anything to harm you. You must believe me.'

Is that what you told your first three husbands? Go on, pack your bags and get out.'

As he watched the gold-digger leave in a taxi, Marcus smiled. He had just saved his father from making a big mistake.

The day that he should have been married, Joe consoled himself with a bottle of whisky inside his locked garage. Broken-hearted, he started the car engine.

A few days later, with tears streaming down her face, Sharon McIntyre read about the suicide of the first man she had ever truly loved, the only man who had truly seemed to care for her.

Two months later, Marcus and Kirsty attended the reading of their father's Will. The solicitor explained.

'Your father's Will was made "in contemplation of marriage". Sadly, the first part of the Will cannot now be enforced.'

'Can you just cut to the chase?' said Marcus. 'I have a pile of bills to pay.'

'If you insist. The residue of your father's estate is to be shared equally between his children, that is, of course, Kirsty and yourself.'

'I know that, but how much have we got?'

'The residue is shared after your father's debts are settled and taxes paid.'

'Father didn't have any debts – did he?'

'The bank has foreclosed on the family business.'

'But we still have the house, don't we?'

'I'm afraid not. The house was security for the business.'

'So how much will we be left with when it's sold?'

'Your father re-mortgaged up to the hilt to pay for his divorce and shore up the business. I'll sort out the paperwork, but if I were you, I'd start looking for a place to live, because there will be next to nothing left.'

Clearing out his late father's desk, Marcus found an invoice from a private detective agency. Why on earth would Dad use a private detective? He gave them a call.

'Hello, can I speak to Howard Winstanley?'

'At your service, what can I do for you?'

'You did some work for my father, Joseph Davis.'

'That's right, I remember, a most unusual job.'

'I'm his son, Marcus. Unfortunately, my father has died. What do you mean, "a most unusual job"?'

'He asked me to find him a wealthy widow who could look after him and his kids because his business was going down the pan. I found him a woman who already owned three properties and had three lots of inheritance in the bank; he even paid me a bonus. Said she was a looker, too.

'Strangest job I've ever been asked to do. Most Gold-diggers are female.'

+++++

Thinking Outside the Box

Sometimes we men just refuse to let go. Maybe it's a Y-chromosome thing? With each mouthful of drink, I had tried to drown my sorrows, but hope surfaced and built a raft that morphed into a gondola and we were back together again, holding hands and counting stars.

I knew every curve of the coast road to her house, just like I knew every curve of her body, and I knew that if we talked things over, I could make everything better. It was a stupid decision, one that I will regret for the rest of my life. I had driven past that tree a hundred times before but tonight, as I struggled to find relationship-mending words, it hit me right between the eyes, literally. Funny, isn't it, how a little thing like your heart breaking can distract you from the important things in life?

As I count the stars through the shattered windscreen, the sea-breeze caresses my blood-stained face. She said I was lame with no feelings and I have proved her right. The pains in my shattered legs are easing now, which is probably not a good sign because when you feel pain, you know you are still alive. She said I was dead from the neck up and soon, she will be proved right again.

She never really loved me, I realise that now. I wonder, will my family arrange a cremation, or a burial?

She said that I never thought outside the box.

Well, she got that wrong.

Easy, Tiger

No amount of training can prepare you for the real thing, thought 20-year-old volunteer zoo assistant Billy, as Arthur took charge of a rifle and enough tranquiliser darts to fell an elephant. Billy cursed his luck. Tonight, he had a hot date with Zoe from the canteen, a tigress in bed by all accounts.

'Do you think this is a drill, Arthur? Only I hadn't planned to die this young.'

Arthur loaded his rifle. 'Stick with me, lad, I'm a trained marksman.'

Billy used to be wild about animals, but his enthusiasm was fading fast. 'Could it be an elephant that's escaped?'

'Not on your Nellie. The message "Code Red" implies it's a dangerous predator; it's probably a big cat.'

The radio crackled again: *Escaped animal is a tiger. Locate and report position.*

'Told you so.' Arthur raised his rifle and looked down the barrel and through the sight. 'I've always wanted to shoot a big cat.'

'Hang on Arthur, didn't the radio say: "Locate and report position"?'

'Where's the sport in that, Billy? This is my big chance to put years of training into practice, so just keep your eyes peeled. If it's male, it's 1.7 to 2.5 metres long; female, 1.4 to 1.7 metres long, and stop those knees from knocking.

Billy now understood how it felt to be an endangered species.

What's that over there?' said Arthur, 'behind that tree?' Jutting out from behind a tree was a striped backside and tail.

'That fur looks more "Tigger" than tiger...' whispered Billy.

Arthur sank to one knee, raised his rifle, steadied himself, and took careful aim.

'...and why is the tiger standing on its hind legs?'

Another radio message: *Tiger is female. Locate and report position.*

Arthur began to squeeze the trigger. 'I've got you now, my beauty,' he cried.

'OH MY GOD, STOP!' shouted Billy, but he was too late.

Arthur fired.

Billy removed the costume-head from the victim. Inside was Zoe, a tigress in bed, by all accounts.

+++++

This story was inspired by a newspaper article about a zoo in China where an employee ran around in a tiger outfit, tracked by 'marksmen' during an emergency procedures rehearsal, much to the amusement of zoo visitors.

Memory

I remember The Beano,
Buster and The Dandy.
Nobby Stiles, Geoff Hurst
and of course Sir Alf Ramsey.

The Lulu Show, Top of the Pops,
Ready, Steady, Go,
and for some strange reason,
Barry Manilow.

Miners went on strike,
man walked on the moon.
Kennedy was shot, and
Uri Geller bent a spoon.

Green Shield stamps, Luncheon Vouchers,
I saved them all.
I laughed at Morecombe and Wise
but not Cannon & Ball.

I watched Happy Days and
Doctor Who and the Daleks.
I played British Bulldog,
Conkers and Jacks.

Our greasy-spoon cafe had a
pinball machine and juke box.

I remember The Sun and page 3,
especially Samantha Fox.

I remember hippies, flower power,
free love and afro hair.
Wild parties with LSD, séances,
spin the bottle and truth or dare.

Those were the days, I kid you not,
skirts were mini and pants were hot.
Did you ever hitch-hike down to the coast?
Or enjoy the delights of Marmite on toast?

Boys wore Levi jeans,
tank-tops or kipper ties.
And we bought our cigarettes
in packets of five.

We were one or the other,
a mod or a rocker.
We loved The Who, Bob Dylan,
and even Joe Cocker.

Rockers wore blue suede shoes
or toe-crushing winklepickers.
Mods wore checked suits,
or Union Jack-covered parkas.

Most girls wore mini-skirts,
hot-pants or trouser suits.

But others cropped their hair
and wore bovver boots.

Most girls drank Babycham
or lager and lime.
Others drank rum and black,
cider or barley wine.

I remember the Mersey sound,
rock & roll, even punk rock.
I saw the Stones in Hyde Park,
and Jimmy at Woodstock.

A hand touched my shoulder.
'Brian, it's time for your medication.'
I said, 'Nurse, live your life to the full,
it's a goddamn celebration.

'Because one day,
you may end up just like me.
And all you'll have left
is memory.'

+++++

The Birds and the Bees

'Mummy, where do babies come from?'

The question, for all its simplicity, sent a chill down Janet's spine and struck fear into her heart. 'Why on earth do you want to know that?'

'Tommy said that his mummy's got a new baby.'

'Well, maybe we can go and see it one day. Now, what would you like for breakfast? I've got Special K or Coco Pops.'

'I wanna baby!'

Janet, a modern mother, planned to tell the truth, no matter how difficult the situation. 'Well, er, babies are, kind of, made, by two people who are in love.' She regretted the little white lie immediately.

'I love you, Mummy, can we make a baby?'

'No, don't be silly, it has to be a boy and a girl.'

'I know *that*, Mummy, *all* babies are boys or girls.'

'No, what I mean is…' She paused in order to formulate a truthful explantion. '…babies are made by a boy and a girl, when they are in love.' The little white lie had slipped out again.

'I love Tommy, can I make a baby with him?'

'Certainly not! Anyway, you have to be grown up.'

'But I am grown up, look.' Emily lifted her dress to show off her big girl's pants.

This was becoming difficult. Janet took a deep breath. 'Tommy's new baby was made when his daddy slept with his mummy and put seed in her belly.' There, that wasn't so bad, was it; a good, honest explanation.

'But Tommy doesn't have a daddy, he has two

mummies.'

Janet had completely forgotten about Tommy's unusual parental situation, even though it was the hot gossip at the school gates, and now wished that she had spoken about tadpoles, or storks, or the birds and the bees.

'Do you want milk on your Coco Pops?' she asked, desperately trying to change the subject, but Emily was not finished yet.

'Where do the seeds come from, Mummy?'

Janet's mind had gone blank. She sipped coffee to calm her nerves. 'Eat your Coco Pops.'

Emily looked up from her cereal. 'Shall I ask one of Tommy's mummies if they have some seed left?'

Janet sprayed a mouthful of coffee across the kitchen table. 'Emily! You'll do no such thing. Trust me on this, they won't have any seed left.'

Emily put on her, 'I know you're not telling me everything' expression, and tried to put the pieces of information together for herself. 'So, when you and Daddy sleep together - because you are in love - do you - make the seed - that makes - a baby?'

'Yes, Emily, that's right. Well done. Now get your coat, let's not be late for school.' That went well, thought Janet, sipping her coffee.

'So will you and Daddy make a baby tonight?'

Janet sprayed another mouthful of coffee over the table. 'Well, sweetheart, it doesn't always work out like that. Sometimes we have to try lots of times before we make a baby.'

'So, where does the baby come out?'

Janet was sinking fast and scrambling for a lifejacket. Desperate times required desperate measures. 'Where did Tommy say the baby comes out?'

'From the belly-button.'

'Well he's wrong,' said Janet, feeling victorious for persevering with the truth; 'they come out from your – er – all ladies – er – we have a special place.'

To Janet's relief, Emily seemed satisfied at last.

Proud of the way she had handled a difficult situation with honesty, give or take a few white lies, Janet hummed merrily as she sorted out the laundry upstairs. She heard the front door open, and heard Emily's delight at her father's return from work. 'Daddy, Daddy,' squealed Emily, rushing into his arms.

He lifted her up and swung her around, before returning her to ground level. 'And what have you learned today, my angel?'

Upstairs, Janet smiled contentedly.

'Mummy's upstairs and she wants some of your seed to make a baby, and she said you may have to try lots of times...' Janet dropped laundry everywhere. '...and Daddy...'

'Yes, my angel?'

'I know about Mummy's special place...'

'Y-you do?'

'...and Daddy, Tommy's two mummies need some more seed, so will you save some for them...'

Janet reached the foot of the stairs just as Emily asked her final question.

'...and Daddy...'

'Yes, my angel?'

'...please can I watch?'

+++++

71

By Mutual Consent

Jane was approaching 40 years of age from the wrong direction, but with the help of designer clothes and carefully applied make-up, she could still turn heads. No matter how bad life became, and it had been pretty bad the last few years, there was always shopping. She said a little prayer: 'Armani, who art in heaven, hallowed be thy name,' as she rifled through her vast wardrobe. Her fingers settled on her little black dress. It was short, low-cut and split up the sides. Together with her red stilettos, it was the perfect choice. She drank another vodka, before slipping into the dress. It fitted like a glove.

It had been a joint decision. They both wanted to add spice to a stale relationship, although Jane suspected that she was far more enthusiastic than her husband. Eventually, they both agreed that on Saturday nights, so long as it was done out of town, they were free to experiment.

Mitch was slobbed out on the sofa, half watching football on the TV, as Jane sneaked out the front door to the waiting taxi. As the taxi-driver gave her the once-over, she knew her choice of outfit was right.

'Where to, miss?' he asked, adjusting his interior mirror so that he could watch her, and not the traffic.

'To the Sheridan Hotel, James,' she ordered, as if

addressing her butler, 'and don't spare the horses.' She felt alive and excited, and the fixed gaze of the taxi-driver added to her delight. She deliberately crossed, then un-crossed her legs, causing the taxi-driver to swerve.

'Shouldn't you be watching the road?'

The Sheridan was a drab hotel, but the ideal location. It was rarely frequented by residents of the area, it was out of town and because of its conference suites, it was often filled with businessmen attending courses.

Sure enough, as she entered the hotel and walked to the bar, most of the businessmen present sucked in their stomachs and glanced her way. For a moment, Jane thought about Mitch slobbed out on the settee in front of the TV. She was a serial bad-decision maker, and Mitch was certainly one of her biggest mistakes.

She eased herself onto a bar stool, ordered a vodka and tonic, and thought about something her mother taught her. *Men are so predictable. They only have two emotions: horny and hungry. If you see a man without a hard-on, make him a sandwich.*

She turned her attention back to the two men who were approaching her. 'Well hello, boys, do you want a sandwich?'

'Only if you're in the middle,' said the taller of the two, 'Can we buy you a drink?'

'Sure, a vodka and tonic would be nice.'

He turned to the listening barman, 'and two pints of bitter, plus one for yourself.'

Jane glanced around the bar, sipping her second drink.

'So what's a nice girl like you doing in a place like this?' the taller man continued, halitosis hitting her right between the eyes. 'My name's Hal.'

Halitosis Hal; that should be easy to remember.

'And my name's Tommy,' said the shorter of the two, nervously.

Jane sipped her drink some more. She knew it was risky dressing like a whore and visiting a strange bar, but it was Saturday night, and she was here by mutual consent. She glanced at her Rolex watch.

'I'm waiting for my boyfriend, but it looks like I've been stood up.' She watched the look the two men exchanged.

'We'll keep you company won't we, Tommy.'

'If you don't mind, miss.'

They were not what she was looking for, and she decided to put them out of their misery. 'Do your wives know you chat up women in hotel bars?'

Tommy turned to Hal as they walked away, 'See, I told you it was a waste of time.'

Another man approached her, dressed in a bow-tie and dinner suit, and many of the men in the hotel bar watched to see how long he would last.

'Hi, my name's Shane. I hope you know CPR, love, because you've just taken my breath away.'

Janet smiled. 'Is that the best line you could think of?'

I've never been good with words, but I am good with my hands.' His hands fell to her thighs and squeezed them gently.

She removed his hands. 'Let's not get ahead of ourselves.'

'I know what you're doing, perched on that bar stool flashing stocking tops and cleavage to anyone who looks your way. It's all a game, isn't it?' He replaced both his hands on her thighs, leaned forward, and kissed her lips. 'I bet your husband's here right now.' Jane's excitement was at fever-pitch. She was like a junkie and she needed her fix.

He led her outside into the car-park, pinned her up against a tree, and paused to see if anyone would come to rescue her.

Her heart was racing fast, it was Saturday night, she was here by mutual consent, and everything was working out as planned.

He relaxed his grip on her arms and planted another kiss on her waiting lips before kissing her neck and reaching for the hem of her dress. As a gentle breeze caressed her thighs, she stopped him from going any further.

'Wait, not here. Let's go back to my place.'

She led him to her front door. 'Shh, we have to be quiet; we don't want to wake Mitch. He'll more than likely be asleep on the settee. Follow me, quietly; my bedroom is up the stairs, on the left.'

They crept up the stairs and as soon as they were inside her bedroom, their passions boiled over. They tore each other's clothes off and made mad, passionate love. As their passions subsided, it was Jane who noticed him first. Mitch was watching them from the open doorway.

'Mitch, get out,' she screamed. But he was going

nowhere. His size cast a large shadow over the double bed and a crooked smile played across his face. He was panting now, and a smell of gas invaded the bedroom.

Eyes smarting from the methane gas, the two lovers dived under the bedclothes as Mitch launched himself onto the bed.

In the claustrophobic darkness under the bedclothes, Jane turned to her husband. 'Two things, Shane: first of all, Mitch will have to go, I don't know why we chose a St Bernard, and second, don't leave it so late next time before you come to my rescue. Halitosis Hal and his sidekick were beginning to look quite attractive.'

+++++

50-WORD MINI SAGAS

Heaven Help Me

'Heavenly Father, so far today, I have not uttered profanities, taken illegal drugs, placed a bet or watched pornography on the Internet; nor have I harboured evil thoughts about friends and family. But now, Lord, I really need your help, because it's time for me to get out of bed.'

The Good Samaritan

A pastor noticed a very small boy trying to press a doorbell on a house across the street. However, the doorbell was too high for him to reach.

The pastor helped, giving the doorbell a solid ring.

'And what now, my friend?'

To which the boy replied, 'Now we run!'

An E-mail From God

One day God sent an angel down to earth to monitor humans. When she returned she told God, '95% are doing evil, 5% are doing good.'

So he decided to e-mail the 5% that were doing good.

Do you know what the e-mail said? No? So you didn't get one either?

A ONE ACT PLAY

Speed Dating
for the Over 50's

Seated at the table is Betty, who speaks in a poorly disguised, fake, Somerset accent.

ANNOUNCEMENT: Gentlemen, you have 10 minutes at each table. Your time starts...now (ding dong).

Major   Good evening madam, my name is Major, may I sit down? Well, speed dating for the over 50's, that's a bit of an oxymoron.

Betty   'Ere, who you calling a moron?

Major   What I mean is, the phrase speed dating for the over 50's, it's like the phrase, military intelligence, the words contradict themselves, don't you think? Perhaps it should be called, slow dating for the over 50's; after all, when was the last time that you used speed?

Betty   'Ere, I don't do drugs, I don't.

Major   What I meant was speed, as in doing something fast.

Betty   'Ere, I takes paracetamol, I do.

Major   I beg your pardon?

Betty   Oh, and poo tablets when I gets the squirts.

Major   I'm sorry, but you've lost me. What *are* you talking about?

Betty   Drugs, you asked me if I used speed.

Major   No I didn't, I meant... Oh, never mind... *(looks at badge)* ...Betty, what's Betty short for?

Betty   It runs in the family, it do.

Major   The name Betty runs in the family?

Betty   Course not! Being short runs in the family, you asked what I was short for.

Major   No, what I said was, what's Betty short for?

Betty   'Ere, you're not so tall yerself... *(squints at his name badge)* ...Major.

Major   *(puffing out chest)* I'll have you know, I'm six feet tall in my bare feet.

Betty   In your bear feet. 'Ere, you in the circus?

Major   I mean b-a-r-e, bare, not b-e-a-r, bear.

Betty   'Ere, I think it's cruel, I do.

Major   And what are you talking about now?

Betty   They should ban them circus's they should.

Major   Are you doing this on purpose, or is there really something wrong with your hearing?

Betty   Something wrong with me earrings? *(feels ear-lobes)* 'Ere, I ain't wearing no earrings.

Major   That's enough! You're doing this on purpose – and will you please stop using that ridiculous fake Somerset accent? Are you doing this just for attention?

             Betty jumps up and salutes

Major   And what are you doing now?

Betty   'Ere, you said attention, so I thought, you being a major an' all...'

Major   *(folding arms)* You'll have to do better

than that. You're putting on an act, your a masquerader.

Betty   *(twists neck)* Where? I don't see no masked raider.

Major   Is your hearing defective?

Betty   A detective? Where? *(twists neck)* Is he chasing the masked raider?

Major   Oh, this is futile.

Betty   'Ere, there's no need to swear.

Major   And I bet your name's not Betty, either!

Betty   Betty Either? Oh no, my name's Betty Marshall, it be.

Major   It be! It be! What kind of language is that? I can see right through you, Betty, and why is one of your breasts six inches lower than the other?

Betty   'Ere, you leave my breasts alone *(juggles breasts)*

Major   And don't think I haven't noticed – you're not even a proper woman!

Betty   'Ere, just because I don't talk proper like

what you do – don't mean I'm not a proper woman, it don't.

Major   You're a fraud. Isn't your conscience even a little pricked?

(pause as Betty rubs her chin and looks at audience)

Betty   'Ere, I can't think of a reply to that one.

Major   I'm going to report you to the organisers.

ANNOUNCEMENT: Ding dong – please change tables

Betty   It was nice meeting you Major. Good luck at your next table.

Major   Oh no you don't. Sit down *(turns)* No, I'm not changing tables... I don't care... go away. *(turns back)* Now, where were we? Oh yes, what are you playing at?

Betty   *(without accent)* It's a fair cop. My name's Bill, but at least I lasted ten minutes.

Major   You mean you dressed up as a woman just for fun?

Betty/Bill   Sorry if you were looking for Mrs Right, Major, but yes, I did it for a laugh, but it's definitely a one-off. *(juggles false*

82

breasts) I think I'll stick to being a man. After all, we have all the advantages.

Major   What advantages? Pray tell?

Betty/Bill   Well for a start, a man can go to the toilet without a support group, and the size of our 'ass' is not a factor in a job interview. So tell me, are you a real major?

Major   Well – no – but...

Betty/Bill   So why pretend to be one? Do women go weak at the knees and throw their corsets at you?

Major   At least I'm trying to make conversation, all you've done is act the fool.

Betty/Bill   There you go again, talking down to me. At least I'm an honest fool, and not a sexual predator preying on the blue-rinse brigade. Sex is not important to me anymore. In fact it's been so long since I did it, I can't remember who ties up who.

Major   It's not about sex, it's not that at all.

Betty/Bill   What is it then? You really should get out from behind your mask. When was

	the last time you got drunk, or told a joke?
Major	Well – er...
Betty/Bill	Look. It's easy. My wife is so immature. Once I was having a bath and she came in and sank all my boats. Come on, your turn.

SILENCE

Betty/Bill	Come on, take off your mask. I know you're hiding something.

SILENCE

Betty/Bill	Come on Major, you've no chance of meeting Mrs Right like this. Think of it as free therapy from a stranger.
Major	My grandmother used to say that a stranger is a friend you've yet to meet.
Betty/Bill	She sounds very wise, not like my grandmother. Once, she sat up all night wondering why the sun shone, and then it dawned on her.
Major	You confessed to me earlier; I guess I owe you the same courtesy. I'm not really a major, and my real name is Susan.
Betty/Bill	*(leans forward)* How do you get your make up as good as that? Come on Sue, what's your story? Are you a transvestite? Bisexual? I have a mate who's bisexual,

when he wants sex, he buys it.

Major/Sue   I don't know what to say.

Betty/Bill   Say what you like. *(changes to a Somerset accent)* – I'm just a stranger on a very strange night. Ere, I reckon it must be one of them full moons, I do.

SILENCE

Betty/Bill   Whatever you say will go in one ear and out the other. That reminds me, I'm not saying that my ex-wife was empty-headed, but if you stood really close to her, you could hear the sea. Do you get it?

Major/Sue   Yes, I get it. You're funny in a strange sort of way.

Betty/Bill   I tell you what, let's forget the serious stuff, we've all got our problems, let's just have a laugh instead. Come on, make me laugh.

Major/Sue   I'm not really in a laughing mood, but I did read something in the papers the other day about a clown who was unjustly sacked from the circus.

Betty/Bill   *(with accent)* 'Ere, I hate circuses, I do. So what happened to that there clown what was unjustly sacked?

Major/Sue   *(smiling)* He sued for funfair dismissal.

Betty/Bill   *(jumps to his feet and runs around table).* Way to go! Now doesn't that feel better?

Major/Sue   Yes, now will you please sit down?

Betty/Bill   *(with accent)* Ere, do you know how to wipe out a whole circus in one go? Easy, you just go for the juggler!

Major/Sue   To answer your earlier question, I'm not a transvestite, or bisexual. I'm a writer and tonight was research.

Betty/Bill   *(with accent)* 'Ere, how many mystery writers do it take to change a lightbulb?

Major/Sue   *(with accent for the first time)* 'Ere, I don't know. How many mystery writers do it take to change a lightbulb?

Betty/Bill   *(with accent)* Two. One screws the bulb in, the other gives it a surprise twist at the end!

Major/Sue   Ha ha! So, what do you do in the real world?

Betty/Bill   I used to hold an important post at Battersea Dogs Home. Oh, and I used to be a werewolf, but I'm all right nowwww *(howls loudly).*

Major/Sue   *(touches his arm)* Shhh. You really are the

most terrible company. Before our time is up, I'd just like to say, behind your endless jokes, I don't believe you're happy. You're just a clown, hiding behind your make up.

Betty/Bill Quid pro quo. I'd just like to say, all you need is a complete personality transplant, medication, electric shock treatment and many years of therapy ...

ANNOUNCEMENT: Ding dong, please change tables

Betty/Bill I know. Let's get out of here with a bang. *(stands up and speaks loudly with accent)* Did you just say, 'will you marry me'?

Major/Sue That's correct. Yes or no?

Betty/Bill *(links arms and speaks with accent)* 'Ere, course I will major, long as you puts a ring on me finger. *(loud applause around the room)* – *(whispers)* – let's get out of here *(jiggles false breasts)* this bra's killing me.

Major/Sue *(as they leave the stage)* Now that we're engaged, we should go on a proper date.

Betty/Bill I know just the place. There's this new restaurant called The Moon; the foods good; it just lacks a bit of atmosphere.

+++++

Morning Has Broken

*There is something truly magical
about the early morn,
in my south-facing garden,
as I stretch and yawn.*

*Not even the scent on the wind,
of cows in nearby fields
can dampen the enthusiasm
and optimism I feel.*

*Apart from a whistling paperboy
busy on his round,
Mother Nature's dawn chorus
is the only audible sound.*

*Fish in the pond sense my presence,
and most of them rise to the top.
For pellets, bread or fish flakes,
to them it matters not.*

*Two jets scratch the clear blue sky,
as the sun removes the morning chill.
Shrubs shiver in a light breeze,
that shakes both tulip and daffodil.*

Alas, this vision of paradise
never lasts for very long.
All the birds have now flown,
and with them went their song.

The goldfish are on the bottom,
by far the safest place.
In case a beer can or football,
lands on the pond surface.

They heard my neighbour's son,
about the same time as me.
Unfortunately, he's carved
from the unsociable tree.

He stands now in his garden,
for his early morning cough.
Talking loud on his mobile phone,
every second word is 'off'.

He clears his throat of phlegm,
then spits it on the floor.
I go back inside my house,
and securely lock my door.

Morning has broken.

+++++

Visitors Are a Blessing

The doorbell rang several times. Bill looked up from his newspaper. 'Well, aren't you going to answer it?'

'Sssh, they'll go away in a minute.'

'It might be your mother.'

Mary looked daggers at her husband. 'You know she's been dead for almost ten years.'

'But tonight's the night of the undead, and it's a full moon, so you never know.'

Mary peeked through a chink in the drawn curtains. 'It's a bunch of kids, and they're going now.'

'I thought you Christians were supposed to be charitable? Halloween is only a bit of fun.'

'This has nowt to do with charity. Halloween is a pagan ritual that has been hijacked by money-hungry companies. This is organised crime; the parents of these kids need locking up. I refuse to encourage them.'

The doorbell rang again, and Mary peeked once more through the curtains.

'Mary, was your sense of fun washed away during your baptism?'

'Sssh, it's more blooming kids.'

'No wonder nobody goes to church anymore. Talk about the frozen chosen.'

'You know I like a bit of fun, now and again.'

'Shall *I* be the charitable one and go and give them some sweets?'

'They're already overweight by the looks of them, so not giving them any more sweets *is* being charitable if you ask me. Anyway, we can relax now, those pesky children have gone.'

'Didn't your God say, "Let those pesky children come unto me"?'

Mary peeked out of the curtains again. 'The street looks clear now; perhaps all the little beggars are full up.'

'In many countries around the world, visitors are seen as a blessing, Mary, but obviously not here at 26 Primrose Mansions.'

The following evening, the doorbell rang several times. Bill looked up from his newspaper. 'Well, aren't you going to answer it?'

Mary opened the front door and began talking to people on the doorstep. Bill strained his ears but only caught the end of the conversation as his wife said, 'Please, do come in.'

Bill put down his newspaper and stood up politely as she led four strangers into the lounge.

'Bill, these four salespeople are cold and wet and I said you'd make them a cup of tea. After all, here at 26 Primrose Mansions, *all* visitors are a blessing.' She kissed a startled Bill on the cheek. 'I'm off to choir practice, I'll see you later.'

As Mary shut the door behind her, Bill asked the group to sit down. 'Oh, is that your brochure? Let me have a look.'

'With pleasure. We call it *The Watchtower.*'

Worlds Apart

Tuesday 9th August 2011

BRISTOL, 3am: The front windows of the Thomas Sabo jewellery store were smashed by one of many gangs looting in Bristol city centre. 'Go, go, go,' urged Tracey, unable to join in the looting because she was on probation; 'keep your hoods up and your heads down, grab what you can, and be quick.'

Daughters Zoe and Kim ran quickly through the smoke from burning cars, stepped carefully over broken glass, and joined looters already in the store. Police, as they had the previous night during riots in London, stood back and let the looting take place.

Zoe muscled her way between other looters grabbing watches and jewellery, one necklace snapping in a tug of war, sending stones flying through the air. Fourteen-year-old Kim had found a beautiful necklace and, just for a second, lowered her hood to try it on. That would make the ideal present for Zoe's sixteenth birthday she thought, replacing her hood. Kim was first to return to her mother; Zoe followed minutes later.

By the time police moved forward to protect what was left of the store, Tracey and her daughters had disappeared into the night.

'Everything on the table,' ordered Tracey, once they were home. Zoe put several items on the kitchen table, but Kim only a few, explaining that she did get her hands on a gold watch, but someone stole it from her.

She kept Zoe's birthday present a secret.

The back door opened with a groan, giving the children a start, but Tracey knew who it was. 'Get to bed, girls, you've done well.'

'Some of us have,' laughed Zoe.

Thirty minutes later, after tough haggling, Freddie left the way he came, through the back door and down the alley, heading to his next appointment. Tonight was a good night to be a fence.

NAIROBI, 3am: Plastic containers strategically positioned around the mud hut had caught some overnight rain from the tin roof. Today, at least, they would start the day clean. Thirty-year-old Grace struggled to her feet and washed her body, using as little of the precious water as possible, before waking her daughter, 14-year-old Razalder.

The sun blinked low and orange between the trees that bordered the dusty road as they started their four-hour walk to the textile factory 20 kilometres away. Grace remembered when her father died 15 years ago, leaving her mother to care for four young children. Being the eldest, Grace dropped out of school to help support the family and found work in the textile factory just outside Nairobi. The hours were long and the wages poor.

She remembered even more vividly the day her daughter was conceived. It was her second day at the factory. Midges hovered around the bare lightbulbs over the workstations as she worked the treadle sewing machine, dreaming of one day finishing school and going on to university. The heat was intense from the tropical sun that beat down on the tin roof, and the sour smell of body odour hung over the workers crammed into the small factory.

Lamek the foreman had taken a shine to her. 'I wanted to make you know, Grace, I can fix you for more hours. You like double-time, yes?' Grace was overjoyed: a job, double time and a man friend; this was better than school, she thought, until Lamek raped her in his office.

Halfway to the factory, Grace and Razalder stopped to rest their aching limbs. The lament of distant drums was drowned out by a petrol tanker belching out fumes as it struggled past them, its wheels kissing the red earth, sending plumes of red mist into the air.

Soon they were back on their feet, and using a walk perfected through generations, they walked side-by-side with straight backs, conserving energy for the long shift ahead. The factory had a large order for imitation Gucci jackets, and they dared not be late.

BRISTOL, 6pm: Tracey had never worked a day in her life. Pregnant at 16, she soon learned the benefits of social security. A second child increased the size of her cheques and earned her a council house. Kim, her youngest, struggled to keep pace with Zoe, who had quickly learned the art of shoplifting. Tracey was proud of the fact that her children lacked for nothing.

'Please, Mum,' begged Zoe, 'it's only £12 and they still have a few left.'

Tracey knew exactly what Zoe wanted: a replica Gucci jacket as worn by Victoria Beckham. The original cost £3,000, but the supermarket was selling cheap imitations for only £12.

With money in her pocket from the looting, Tracey felt generous. 'Who fancies new gear for Zoe's party?'

As Tracey parked the car, she reminded them both,

'No nickin' stuff; security guards will be on their toes.'

Much to Tracey's annoyance, the entrance to the store was blocked by protesters from the charity War on Want, who waved banners declaring, *Stop slave labour* and *A fair wage for a fair day's work.*

'Before you go into this store,' said a protester, pushing a leaflet into Tracey's hand, 'can I point out that by shopping here, you are encouraging slave labour? Girls about the same age as these,' he said, pointing at her children, 'are working 80 hours a week in desperate conditions for as little as £10 per month.'

'Well, they're bloody stupid, ain't they?'

'Some of them are, but most are desperately poor and exploited, and we need your help to stop it.'

'What's it got to do wiv me? We got politicians to sort out stuff like that, ain't we?'

She shoved her way into the store where she treated her kids to new outfits, but despite paying cash, she was stopped at the exit.

'Evening, Tracey,' said the security guard. 'You know the drill. I'm sure you won't mind if we conduct a quick search of you and your family. This way.'

In the privacy of a separate room, Tracey waved her receipt under their noses and their search proved fruitless. One day you'll slip up, the security guard thought, one day.

NAIROBI, 6pm: After ten hours of toil and sweat without a break, many of the factory workers set off home; others stayed on for double time. Grace was HIV positive, another gift from her rape by Lamek the foreman, and was on the verge of collapse.

'Mum, we need the money, so I'll do the double time on my own,' said Razalder. 'You get yourself home and rest. I'll see you later.'

Too tired to argue, Grace left the factory, but walked less than 100 metres before collapsing unconscious in a roadside ditch.

Inside the factory, Vitalis put down the phone. 'Lamek, War on Want come on Friday, yes? Their surprise visit is on. The procedures we have crafted must be used, we must not risk the far we have come. Half the girls must be gone and others need the silence of gold, or they will be in the sack.'

'I know the procedures, Dad. The fire extinguishers from the store, I will get like before, and fire doors will be not locked.'

'Lamek, I thank you for the far we have reached.'

Lamek loved his job, surrounded by females all wanting extra hours. He returned quickly to the machine room. With Grace having left early, Lamek saw his chance for another conquest.

Midges hovered around the bare lightbulbs over the workstations as Razalder worked the treadle sewing machine, dreaming of finishing school and going on to university. The heat was intense from the tropical sun that beat down on the tin roof, and the sour smell of body odour hung over those doing overtime.

Attracted by the smoothness of her olive skin, Lamek the foreman made his move. 'I wanted to make you know, Razalder, I can fix for you more hours. You like double-time, yes?'

BRISTOL, 9pm: In the privacy of her bedroom, Zoe modelled her imitation Gucci jacket before placing it in her packed wardrobe. What she needed now was red hair like Rhianna, and black boots like Britney Spears. It was hard keeping up with fashion, but looking good made her feel good. She opened her top of the range laptop and posted a picture of her wearing her jacket on Facebook.

In another bedroom, Kim threw her new outfit onto the floor. She was fed up with being treated like a child. She lay back on her bed. Maybe when she presented Zoe with the sparkling necklace that was hidden under her pillow, it would change things. Kim dreamt of a better future, of marriage to a footballer or maybe even a pop star who would provide for her so that she wouldn't have to go to work.

NAIROBI, 9pm: As Lamek raped Razalder, the textile factory burst into flames. Locked doors and thick black smoke gave the workers in the machine room little chance of survival. Lamek pushed Razalder onto the office floor and scrambled clear of the building, and watched 30-foot-high flames dance in the night breeze, sending smoke and detritus billowing into the sky. Explosions added to the terror for the few who escaped the inferno.

'What happened?' asked Vitalis.

'I'm not knowing, father, I was in the office room.'

The sound of explosions woke Grace, who was less than 100 metres away. She saw the sky glowing bright red and ran towards the factory and its wall of flames. Her daughter was not amongst the few who had escaped.

Smoke seared her lungs and the heat melted one side of her face as she tried desperately to enter the building. 'Razalder, Razalder,' she shouted.

As Vitalis and Lamek pulled her back, part of the factory roof collapsed with a mighty crash, ending what little chance there was of finding more survivors.

As half a dozen fire engines arrived to battle the flames, Grace sank to her knees in the mud and the smoke beside the burning factory. 'Please, Lord, not my baby, not my baby,' she cried.

BRISTOL, one week later: Tracey and her daughters were woken as their front door was smashed, in one of many early-morning police raids across the city. Gaining entry quickly was crucial in these raids to prevent evidence being destroyed, flushed down the toilet or thrown out of windows.

Within seconds of the forced entry, eight or nine officers invaded the council house and herded the occupants into one room. Before Tracey could protest, a search warrant was shoved in her face. She held Kim close to her chest, instinctively protecting her youngest. 'There's nowt here, you bastards,' she spat, 'and you'll pay for all the damage.'

'Where were you and your daughters at 3am on Tuesday 9th August?'

Tracey played it carefully. 'Was that the night of the riots? We was trying to get home, and got caught up in them riots.'

The officer in charge placed a blurred CCTV photo in front of Tracey, of a young girl trying on a necklace in the Thomas Sabo jewellery store, and spoke directly at the child Tracey was holding. 'And what's your name, I don't think I've had the pleasure?'

'Her name's Kim and if that blurred photo's all you've got, you'll be laughed out of court.'

'Sarge, I've found this necklace under the pillow in the small bedroom.'

The officer in charge smiled. 'Kim Rodgers, I'm

arresting you for looting. You do not have to say anything, but it may harm your defence if you do not mention when questioned something you later rely on in court; anything you do say may be given in evidence. Take her to the car.'

Tracey sank to her knees. 'Please, Lord, not my baby, not my baby,' she cried.

The officer in charge turned around. 'Tracey Rodgers, I'm arresting you on the charge of handling stolen goods. You do not have to say anything, but it may harm your defence if you do not mention when questioned something you later rely on in court; anything you do say may be given in evidence.'

NAIROBI: On the day Tracey and Kim were arrested in England, Grace took a day off from working in the newly-repaired factory to bury her daughter. Most of the village turned out to pay their respects, and all of her family were there, except 15-year-old Benta, who had dropped out of school to take Razalder's place. The desperately poor family now had a funeral to pay for.

It was her second day at the textile factory. Midges hovered around the bare lightbulbs over the workstations as Benta worked the treadle sewing machine, dreaming of finishing school and going on to university. The heat was intense from the tropical sun that beat down on the tin roof, and the sour smell of body odour hung over the workers crammed into the small factory.

Attracted by the smoothness of her olive skin, Lamek the foreman made his move. 'I want to make you know, Benta, I can fix for you more hours. You like double-time, yes?'

Baby Blues

It seemed like a good idea at the time, but I wish I'd never taken the baby now. 'Shh, shh, go to sleep, or I'll not be responsible for my actions.'

If you *were* my baby, my *real* flesh and blood, maybe I would have some sort of mother-baby bond, a maternal instinct, but I haven't, so shut up. Motherhood just isn't in my genes.

What little I remember of my mother before she left proves to me that her skills were zero. What made me think I'd be any different?

This is the deal. I'm gonna rock you until the count of ten, and if you haven't shut up by then, I might just bury you in the back garden. 'One... two... three... four... five... six...' That's better, peace and quiet at last. Maybe you *can* read my mind after all.

We're going to Walmart now, and if you so much as burp in the store; I'll shut you in a freezer and leave you to die.

What you gawping at, I wanna shout, as I carry my baby around the store in a sling, you never seen a young girl with a baby before? What's your problem? Is it because she's Hispanic? Would you smile if my baby was African-American? Why are people so self-righteous and judgemental?

It's my age, isn't it, that's what bothers you. What were you doing at the age of 16? Playing hopscotch, or marbles, or playing doctors and nurses? It's the thought that a young girl has not only played doctors and nurses; she's had an internal examination. That's what you see, isn't it? A whore who got what she deserved, a bun in the oven. Serves her right.

Nobody understands these days why some college girls get lumbered with a baby at 16, because nobody bothers to ask. Permit me to explain.

From a class of 50 students, the tutor chose me to have his baby. I'd never been chosen for anything before and I'll be honest, I felt honoured. I thought having a baby at 16 would be fun, but it isn't.

The feeding, the diapers, the crying, I can just about cope with, but it's the reaction of older people that's the hardest.

Tutors don't consider this when they give out virtual babies at Parenting and Child Development Classes.

I wish I'd chosen psychology now.

+++++

Billy's
'Non-Christmas' Day

Billy opened his eyes on Christmas Day and glanced at his bedside clock. It was 9am. He lifted his head from his pillow and, using both ears, listened for the sounds of movement downstairs; all was quiet. A boyish grin spread across his face. He stretched his six-foot frame and his ten toes appeared from under the blankets, wiggling their annoyance at the chill in the air. He listened once more; not a sound. He savoured the thought for a moment longer, jumped out of bed, and loped over to the window to peep through the curtains; Dad's Morris Minor had gone, leaving just an oil stain on the empty drive. A loud 'yahoo' broke the silence as Billy dived back into bed.

Uncle Alex had inherited a large country mansion in Manchester and wanted to lord it over the rest of the family by showing off his newly acquired wealth. Billy's mum and dad had jumped at the chance of Christmas at someone else's expense, and Billy jumped at the chance to have the house to himself.

He jumped out of bed, and as his pyjama bottoms fell to the floor, he stood to attention, saluting his Lord Kitchener poster. 'I hereby declare today Billy's "non-Christmas" Day, and I further declare there shall be NO mince pies, NO turkey, NO stuffing, NO Queen's Speech and NO sprouts.' He pulled up his pyjamas and jumped back into bed.

Billy had nothing against Christmas, but since leaving school and having worked at the Co-op for 12 consecutive weeks, he'd seen and handled enough mince pies, turkeys, stuffing and sprouts to last him a lifetime.

But the job did have some benefits. Six weeks ago, a young girl dropped a bag of sprouts all over the floor of the Co-op store, and as he helped her recapture them, she captured his heart. Her name was Jessica.

With no parents to cramp his style, the empty house provided the perfect opportunity for him to take their relationship to the next level. All his friends had done it with girls (so they said), and it was time for him to go beyond a peck on the cheek. It was time for a full-on, passionate kiss on the lips. Billy's plans for his non-Christmas Day were simple. First, he would meet Jessica for a lunchtime burger (with no sprouts); second, he would bring her back to the empty house where he would say: *My parents have gone away for a few days. Here's your present.* She would say, *Fab, the Beatles' new single, I can't wait to hear it when I get home,* and he would say, *Let's listen to it now, I have a record player in my bedroom, let's go upstairs and give it a spin.*

He closed his eyes, and imagined the scene. Jessica lay next to him on his bed, and John Lennon was singing, '*I wanna hold your hand.*' He puckered his lips, and leaned forward.

The telephone rang in the hall. Billy opened his eyes – and Jessica was gone.

He trudged downstairs and grabbed the phone.

'Hello? Is that you, Billy? Can you hear me?'

'Yes Mum, I can hear you,' he groaned.

'Is everything OK?'

'Well, Mum, I've singlehandedly chased away two sets of burglars and repelled an alien invasion. Apart from that, it's been pretty quiet.'

'I forgot to tell you, your Christmas present is by the fireplace...' (Billy imagined another knitted reindeer jumper, perfect for a 17-year-old in the swinging sixties), '...and there's plenty of food in the larder.' Billy imagined opening the larder door, only to be crushed to death under an avalanche of mince pies, turkeys, stuffing and sprouts. He needed to end the call quickly. A 'merry you-know-what' would ruin his special day before it had even begun.

'Mum, your voice is fading, I can't hear you – I think the line's playing up – have a good time – bye.' He congratulated himself for his quick thinking. She wouldn't bother calling back for a while if she thought the line was faulty.

He checked his watch. There was still enough time for a record session. To the sound of *She Loves You*, Billy jumped around on his bed, playing an imaginary guitar, but the needle kept jumping out of the grooves of his seven-inch single. Even balancing a coin on the record player's arm did not solve the problem. One day, he vowed, I'll buy myself one of those new stereo record players.

Billy splashed his chin, chest and armpits with Old Spice aftershave before pulling on his Levi jeans. He found a pair of baseball boots, pulled on his favourite *Make Love, Not War* T-shirt, hoping that Jessica would get the hint, and after quickly tidying his bedroom (by shoving stuff under his bed), he grabbed his bomber jacket.

The one present that he really wanted (apart from a new stereo, a Ford Capri and a beard like the bloke out of Manfred Mann) would soon be within his reach.

Billy slid down the banister, swung around the post at the foot of the stairs, found the ten-bob note his mum had left him on the mantelpiece, ignored the suspect present by the fireplace, and prepared to leave the house. He peered out the front bay window. No humans (or aliens) were in sight. Good. A 'merry-you-know-what' was not on his agenda. He crept stealthily out of his front door and, at a quick pace, headed down the street towards the shops. As Billy neared their rendezvous, the roads were deserted, apart from the local police constable on his bicycle.

When Billy first suggested his non-'you-know-what' day, Jessica thought he was mad. She loved Christmas and all its traditions, but a few days ago she had finally agreed to go along with it. What concerned her more was that after six weeks, he still had not given her a passionate kiss. She put on her favourite, flowery-patterned dress and checked her make-up. She traditionally wore a dress on Christmas Day, so Billy would have to lump it.

As she left the house, all she could hear was her mum chopping vegetables in the kitchen.

'Bye, Mum, see you later.'

Jessica was the first to arrive at the burger bar. When

Billy saw her standing in the doorway, he thought all of his 'you-know-what's' had come together. Everything was going like clockwork. As he reached out for a hug, she moved aside, exposing the large red CLOSED sign on the door. 'Looks like burgers are off the menu.'

He should have checked opening times; of course the burger bar would be closed. Quickly, Billy threw together Plan B. 'Never mind, let's go back to my house; there's plenty of food.' He tried to shut out thoughts of what might be lurking behind the larder door.

She poked his ribs playfully. 'OK, but how do I know you can cook?'

'There's only one way to find out – come on.' He grabbed her hand, and they giggled and laughed their way down the street. 'And you're gonna love your present.'

'Oh, Billy, stop. I've forgotten *your* present. I've left it at home on the table. Can we go and get it – *please*?' She fluttered her eyelashes.

Billy decided on a compromise. He was not against the principle of giving and receiving presents, and his curiosity was enough to kill a cat, if not two. 'So what's my present?'

'There's only one way to find out Billy, let's go – come on.'

There was a hint of mischief in her voice as she pulled him in *her* direction. Billy kept looking at her face, trying to read her expression. 'So, we collect my present from your house, and then head straight back to mine?'

'If that's what you want.'

Billy relaxed; that was exactly what he wanted.

They entered Jessica's house. 'Your present's just through here, Billy; come on.' Full of excitement and anticipation, he followed her into the dining room.

Sure enough, his present was on the table. Billy's pupils opened wide, his jaw dropped and his heart sank quicker than the Titanic. His present was not alone. Also on the table were dinner plates, cutlery, Christmas crackers and a plate of mince pies. A familiar smell wafted up his nose. He turned in horror towards the kitchen door and there stood Jessica's mother, carving knife in hand.

'Merry Christmas, Billy; please make yourself at home. With your parents away, we can't have you not eating properly on Christmas Day, now can we? The Queen's Speech will be starting any minute, and dinner won't be much longer. By the way, Billy, do you like sprouts?'

+++++

Meals on Wheels

Underneath a banana tree, they lazed in the shade of the mid-day sun looking forward to the delivery of their food. To the gentle sound of distant drums, they subconsciously moved their heads in time with the beat as they waited patiently for their meal to arrive.

'I'm sick of tasteless local food, I hope we get some nice foreign food today.'

'I know what you mean. I could murder a full English.'

'I saw them taking supplies to the local school earlier, so they should reach here by early afternoon, with any luck.'

'My mouth is watering now; I can almost taste the richness of foreign food. Please, Lord, give the do-gooders the strength to keep feeding us.'

'There's no need for prayers. The Lord knows every hair on our heads, and He will provide all we need. It's just a matter of time.'

They both spotted the tell-tale clouds of red dust in the distance, and made a bee-line towards the vehicle that had now come to a stop. The foreign food was here at last, and it was still warm.

'I don't know how we managed before the white missionaries came,' said one mosquito to the other, as they sank their proboscises into human flesh.

50-WORD MINI SAGAS

World's Worst Practical Joke?

In 2010, when 33 Chilean miners who had been trapped underground for over two months reached the surface, wouldn't it have been funny if the welcome committee including the Chilean president and all the rescuers had been wearing *Planet of the Apes* fancy dress costumes?

On second thoughts, perhaps not.

A Woman Scorned

It was obvious from the way that he caressed her body that she was his new love. Full of jealousy, his wife grabbed the carving knife and slashed her again and again, plunging the knife in up to the hilt.

Wheezes of dying breath escaped as the Jaguar tyres deflated.

You Look Fine!

I think what you're wearing is fine just like what you wore five minutes ago was also fine. Either pair of shoes is fine. With the belt is fine. Without it is fine, too. Your hair is fine. Your make-up is fine. You look fine. Can we please just go?

Happy Anniversary, Darling

As she regained consciousness, she glowered at her husband who towered over her. 'So help me God, the next time you hit me, I'll kill you.'

'And the next time my tea is burned, I'll kill you; you'd burn a salad, given half the chance.' Fred Smith stepped over the broken plate that littered the kitchen floor. 'I'm off down the pub.'

'Bloody good riddance,' his wife shouted. After hearing the front door slam, she eased herself off the floor and into a chair. A glass of vodka did little to help ease the pain of an abusive and loveless marriage. The army had turned him into a monster. Thank God we don't have children.

In the bar, Fred listened intently to the loudmouth holding court nearby. 'On-line chat-rooms, that's the place to go for fun; loads of women all looking for "relationships". I've got three on the go at the moment.' His phone vibrated on the bar. 'Gotta go, that's number two, ready and waiting for some TLC.'

Fred finished his pint, and followed him out the door. 'So these chat-rooms: does anything go?'

'Within reason,' laughed the loudmouth.

Three pints later, Fred returned home. He could hear her before he opened the front door. Nora the snorer, as he called her, snored louder than a pneumatic drill. Her snoring was so bad, they had separate bedrooms. Even their neighbours had complained!

Nora was asleep on the sofa with a half-empty bottle of vodka by her side. He entered his bedroom and shut the door, slightly reducing the annoying sound from downstairs. He flicked on his computer and poured himself a drink. Sleep did not come easy when he came home on leave; that's the army for you.

He searched 'internet chat-rooms'. 67 million options including: *be naughty, illicit encounters, up for it, lonely wives, teen rooms, drinking, party, singles, passion, click and flirt.* He was in a rut; a bit of fun was just what the doctor ordered.

To a background noise of loud snoring, Fred chose a site, created a user-name, password and an alter-ego named Danny. He didn't know what an avatar was, so he ignored that, and found himself transported into a chat-room within ten minutes.

He poured himself another drink. This could be fun. He posted his first message: *My name's Tommy, I'm an 18 year old soldier off to Afghanistan soon and may not return. I would like to lose my virginity before I die. Any offers?*

The next morning, he fired up his computer and spent hours sifting through messages. He was surprised by the high number of gay responses. He decided that he needed some advice.

Nora paced nervously in the kitchen. Should she offer him some breakfast? At mid-day, he came downstairs. 'Don't worry about food; I'm off down the pub.'

'What you been doing on the computer?'

'Been listening at the door have you? Mind your

own business. I'm off down the pub for a few hours.'

As he slammed the front door behind him, Nora breathed a sigh of relief and reached for her bottle of vodka. She tested the weight of the bottle in her hands and wondered if one mighty blow on the back of his head would cave in his skull. If it didn't, he would surely kill her.

Fred Smith nursed his pint, waiting for the chat-room loudmouth, and didn't have to wait long.

'Hi, my name's Fred; can I buy you a drink? I want to pick your brains about chat-rooms.'

'Sure, a pint of bitter, please, although I must warn you, I'm no expert. What do you want to know?'

'How well are chat-rooms policed?'

'There are thousands of sites and millions of messages. As long as you don't use your real name and are password protected, you can stay below the radar, unless of course you are a complete deviant, and download or post bad stuff, like...'

'Oh no, I'm not a pervert, I'm just after some fun.'

'You'll find plenty of that, that's for sure.'

Fred smiled. 'Thanks for your help.'

When Fred arrived home, his wife was snoring loudly on the settee, an empty bottle of vodka by her side. He tip-toed upstairs and closed his bedroom door.

Nora, only pretending to be asleep, listened at the foot of the stairs to the bleep of his computer as he turned it on. Why the sudden interest?

Fred, aka Tommy, posted again. *Why are all the good girls taken?* That message should reduce the number of posts from gay men. He poured himself a Jack Daniel's, then bit into a sandwich. He posted again. *I'm just a lonely, sensitive guy, going to war.*

Messages continued to flood in and one caught his eye from Emma. *Hey soldier boy, you really a virgin? Got ginger hair or summat?*

Tommy replied, *Are you psychic? It's my ginger hair that scares all the nice girls away.*

Emma replied immediately, *I'm not a nice girl.*

Tommy's heartbeat quickened; this was fun. *Are you fit?*

Emma replied, *Had no complaints so far, carrot top.*

Nora listened to the tapping of the keys from outside his bedroom door. She dared not open it; instead she knocked. 'Do you want anything?'

All images of his fantasy girlfriend Emma disappeared with the knock on the door. For a moment, he panicked like a man caught red handed with his pants down.

'Do you want anything?' repeated Nora.

'Not you, that's for sure. Just clear off and leave me alone.'

As Fred's obsession grew, so did Nora's curiosity. His behaviour settled into a routine and when he sloped off to the pub, Nora would relax and pour herself another drink. She started to read the newspaper's problem page. '*My husband is addicted to online porn, what can I do?*' I wonder if that's what he's up to? After peering outside to make sure the coast was clear, she sneaked upstairs into his bedroom and started his computer.

Damn. Password protected. She turned it off and left his bedroom.

She was halfway down the stairs as Fred opened the front door. He eyed her suspiciously. 'You stay out of my bedroom, Nora, you hear? Or you know what you'll get.'

Fred was soon back online in his fantasy world. Emma was everything his wife was not. She was young, witty, cheeky, adventurous and sexy – she wanted him, and he wanted her. What started as light relief was now an infatuation. Fred delved deeper and deeper into his obsession and asked Emma for a date.

Next morning, Nora went shopping. She was more determined than ever to discover his secret. She had a plan that just might work.

Fred returned from the pub and, as usual, found Nora sound asleep on the settee, snoring loudly, an empty vodka bottle by her side. He quickly made a sandwich and was soon back online. Emma had agreed to meet him.

He poured himself a celebration drink. The fact that he was 40 years old would need some explaining, but he was as excited as his alter-ego Tommy, off on his first cyber-date.

Nora had crept up the stairs and waited behind her bedroom door across the landing, vodka bottle in hand.

Fred opened his bedroom door; he needed the toilet. He listened to the sound of snoring echoing up the stairs. 'Drunken cow,' he muttered, 'What did I ever see in her?' Leaving his door open and his computer on, he crossed the landing to the bathroom.

Nora knew she had about 90 seconds. She crept into his bedroom expecting to see porn, but instead read a screen full of messages before slipping back to her hiding place. Fred flushed the loo and returned to the landing. The loud snoring from downstairs brought a smile to his face.

As soon as his bedroom door closed, Nora crept downstairs and stopped the tape recording she had made of her snoring. Not only was he having an affair, he was meeting his girlfriend on Saturday night, their 20th wedding anniversary. You'll pay for this, she vowed.

In another part of town, 35-year-old Beverley looked at her computer screen. Using her alter-ego Emma, she had just arranged a rendezvous with an 18-year-old ginger-haired soldier named Tommy, who would be expecting another teenager. How on earth would she explain?

Saturday evening came and Tommy met Emma in the White Hart as planned. They looked each other up and down.

'Tommy, you're supposed to be 18 years old.'

'Well, so are you, Emma.'

She ruffled his ginger hair. 'Well, at least you didn't lie about this.'

'I'm also not a virgin,' he confessed with a smile.

'Well, now that *is* a surprise,' she laughed. 'I'll let you into a secret, neither am I.'

Despite their mutual deceptions, they had created an online connection and were soon deep in conversation. Holding both of her hands across the table, Tommy leaned forward and gave her a passionate kiss.

Nora arrived at the White Hart Public House 30 minutes later than her husband. He had his back to her and was kissing another woman, but there was no mistaking his head of ginger hair. She raised his army pistol, holding it steady between both hands. 'Happy anniversary darling,' she screamed, and she managed to pump three bullets into him before other customers disarmed her and wrestled her to the ground.

Tommy, aka Fred Smith, turned his unmistakeable head of ginger hair to one side. 'Emma, did you just hear shouting and gunfire?'

Emma, aka Beverley, looked up from her menu in the new restaurant extension on the side of the White Hart Public House.

'Yeah, it sounded like it came from the bar.'

+++++

A Donkey's Tale

'Grandad, will you tell
us a bedtime story,
about the day that earned
you fame and glory?'

'I know that story well,'
I said with a grin.
'Are you lying comfortably in the hay?
Then I will begin.

'By the Grand Pier, we were
positioned in the shade.
Children made sandcastles
with buckets and spades.

'It was half-term and families
didn't have a care
as they played in the sand
at Weston-super-Mare.

'Under knotted hankies,
adults soaked up the sun.
Their children looked around;
they wanted some fun.

"Look, mummy, donkeys,
can we please have a ride?"

117

In those days, kids, a donkey's life
was full of pride.'

'What happened next, Grandad?
asked little Freddie.
Although he'd heard the story
many times already.

'Well, everyone was happy
until they heard a shout.
"Help, I'm stuck in the mud
and I can't get out!"

'Nowadays of course,
if a child was so daft,
a mobile phone would alert
a hovercraft.

But this was back
in the summer of '62,
with little or no prospect
of an easy rescue.

'A concerned crowd gathered,
there seemed little hope.
The boy was sinking as
my keeper brought a rope.'

The young donkeys brayed,
'What happened next?'

'That's when my strength
was put to the test.

'My keeper threw the rope out
with all his might.
"Tie this around your waist, son,
and hold on tight."

'Then he tied to my saddle,
the other end of the rope.
The boy's mother was crying,
she'd given up hope.

'I pulled harder and harder,
the rope stretched tight.
The boy came free from the mud;
oh he did look a sight.

'The Weston Mercury took photos
for a front-page story.
And that's how your grandad
Earned his fame and glory.

'So, how about that then?'
I asked rather proudly.
But the only response
was donkeys snoring loudly.

I lay down in the straw,
and was soon snoring too.
As I remembered that summer's
day in 1962.'

Rules of Engagement

Tom Higgins was a good salesman, his persuasive manner ensuring that he closed more sales than he lost. He had all the trappings of success: a big car, a big penthouse apartment, and a big ego.

At first, he didn't like the idea of Janet going on a 12-month scholarship to America, but it was to do with food, so the long-term benefits should be tastier meals. By e-mail, she had hinted to eating more healthily; some American fad, no doubt.

After a hug and the usual pleasantries on her return, Tom loaded her cases into his brand new BMW and they set off towards home. Apart from the incessant hum of the air-conditioning, all was quiet as Tom manoeuvred through the heavy traffic around the airport.

'I'm glad to have you back, darling; are you hungry?' he asked, relaxing now in lighter traffic. 'Do you want me to stop somewhere on the way home?'

'That would be good. I couldn't eat the airline food, it was disgusting.'

Ten minutes later, they entered Tom's favourite steakhouse where he ordered the largest steak on the menu.

'And what would madam like?' asked the waiter.

'Do you have pumpkin dumplings?'

'No madam, it's just the way I walk,' laughed the knowledgeable waiter. 'How about a nice juicy steak?'

'No, thanks, red meat is bad for you.'

'Red meat's fine,' said Tom. 'It's fuzzy green meat that's bad for you.'

Outnumbered two to one and tired from her long flight, Janet did not have the appetite for an argument, not yet, anyway. 'I'll just have a jacket potato please, with some side salad, and no cheese or mayonnaise.'

'And to drink?'

'Can I have a soya milkshake?'

'It's OK,' Tom explained, 'she's just returned from America. It's like another world out there.'

No it's not, she wanted to scream, it's also full of meat-eating cannibals who like to eat innocent animals.

As soon as the waiter left them, Janet laid her cards on the table. 'Tom, I've become a vegan, and as a consequence, a lover of defenceless animals.'

Just like Don Corleone, Tom lacked compassion. 'I'm also a lover of defenceless animals, especially in a rich gravy. So how long have you followed this craze?'

'It's not a craze.'

The waiter delivered their food and Janet watched in disgust as Tom chewed on a large slice of animal.

'Would you consider giving veganism a try, if I talk you through the benefits?' She knew that Tom becoming a vegan was as unlikely as a washing-machine repair man turning up on the appointed day at the appointed time.

Tom considered her request for all of ten seconds. 'Nothing else has the taste of meat. Man is the only primate that is carnivorous. Eating meat is what made us human.'

Made you inhuman, thought Janet, watching dead cow churn around in his mouth. Janet felt a churning in her stomach and it took all of her will-power not to grab his steak knife and kill him there and then. 'I'll take that as a no then, shall I?'

During the journey home, you could have cut the atmosphere with a steak knife, and Tom was like a dog with a bone. 'Vegan is an old Indian word for lousy hunter. The most enjoyable way to follow a vegetable diet is to let the cow eat it, then eat the cow.'

Janet looked at him the way turkeys look at farmers at Christmas. 'Don't you care about your cholesterol?'

'I drive way too fast to worry about my cholesterol,' he said, accelerating deliberately.

They reached Tom's penthouse apartment and Janet was in a quandary. He had money and he gave her security, but at what price? She decided to end their relationship there and then. As she searched for the right words, Tom jumped out the car, opened the boot, grabbed her cases and headed for the front door. 'Come on, I have a surprise for you inside.'

Janet followed him into his apartment to find it full of beautiful red roses, and on the coffee table an ice bucket contained a bottle of champagne. Tom sank to one knee, reached into his coat pocket and produced a diamond engagement ring. 'Will you marry me?'

Excited and repulsed in equal measures, Janet needed time to think. 'Tom, I'm flattered, I really am, but I'm tired, and we have issues to overcome. Can we do this in the morning? I promise I'll give you an answer tomorrow.'

Tom returned the ring to his pocket. He would win her around to his way of thinking eventually; after all, he was a top salesman. He moved forward for a kiss and Janet gave him a peck on the cheek, shivering at the thought of kissing those lips that had earlier been chewing the flesh of an innocent animal.

'Let's talk tomorrow, Tom, after a good night's sleep.'

Janet lay in bed, deep in thought. Everything was only fine in Tom's world if he made the rules. In America she had learned independence, and she was now a determined, no, more than that, a *radical* vegan. She knew that he would make her life hell until she changed to his way of eating. She decided he could stick his diamond ring where the sun didn't shine. There would be no compromise.

Tom drank another scotch. Things had not gone according to plan; she did not melt into his arms at the airport, she did not swoon over the diamond ring, and they were not together in bed catching up on 12 months of abstinence. Like any objection to a top salesman, this vegan thing would be overcome, somehow.

He slid into bed next to Janet, whose eyes were closed and her breathing constant. He reached out and began to massage her shoulders with soft circular motions; his tender fingers fluttered up and down her spine, just the way she liked it. His fingers slowly released the tensions in her body and she drifted off to sleep. He knew that she had been awake, but he was in no rush. The problem would be easily solved tomorrow.

Up early next morning, Tom quietly dressed and drove to the supermarket to buy vegan-friendly products.

He returned to the bedroom and placed a cup of coffee beside his sleeping girlfriend. 'Janet,' he whispered, rocking her shoulder gently. 'Janet.' She half-opened one eye. 'There's a cup of coffee here if you want it, and I've used soya milk.'

Janet squinted suspiciously at the suspect mug on the bedside cabinet. Tom loved her warmth, her innocence and her child-like vulnerability first thing in the morning. He longed to hold her in his arms, to stroke her blonde hair, and to make her a bacon sandwich.

After he left the bedroom, Janet sat up and sipped her coffee. Sure enough, it was made with soya milk. Could he possibly change?

Feeling encouraged, she entered the kitchen only to crease her nose in disgust at the lingering smell of cooked bacon.

'Sorry about that,' said Tom, holding out a second cup of coffee for her. 'There were two rashers of bacon left and you know how I hate waste. Old habits die hard.'

Young innocent animals die hard, she thought, realising at that precise moment that she would never change him. Does he put down the toilet seat? No. Does he put his dirty clothes in the washing basket? No. Will he stop eating defenceless animals? No.

'Let's go in the lounge and talk things through,' suggested Tom, working softly, softly, towards closure. He reasoned that away from the smell of bacon and surrounded by red roses, her attitude would surely soften.

'So, Tom, when did you buy the soya milk?'

Tom smiled; she was softening already. 'This morning at the supermarket, where a funny thing happened. This girl approached me and said, "Don't I recognise you from vegetarian class?" I was confused; I'd never seen her-bivore.'

Janet was not amused. 'Veganism is no laughing matter, Tom. It's serious, deadly serious.'

'OK, I'm sorry, let's discuss this like civilised people.' He gestured with his right hand. 'After you.'

Despite being surrounded by red roses, Janet spoke her mind. 'A vegan diet is kinder to your health, Tom, kinder to animals, and kinder to the planet.'

'But I read that cow-farts are the leading cause of greenhouse emissions in developed countries, so by eating more cows, we're surely helping the planet.'

'Rubbish! A well-balanced whole-food vegan diet is up there with the healthiest of diets.'

'My ancestors did not scale the evolutionary ladder for me to relinquish the position to carrot-munchers. By eating meat, we carnivores sit as kings at the top of the food chain.'

'But Tom, a vegan diet can improve your quality of life and decrease your chances of diabetes, heart disease and some cancers. It's easy enough to change, and the change could be gradual. In America, I just slowly increased my intake of fruit and vegetables. You could easily do this too.'

Tom discarded his softly, softly approach; winning was all that mattered now. 'Eating meat is what enabled us to move from caves to penthouse apartments. Vitamin B1 is crucial in keeping neural pathways firing and we get it from meat and dairy products. That's why somebody with reduced mental functions is called a vegetable.'

Being labelled a vegetable was the last straw. Janet rose to her feet. 'Sharing meals is an important courtship ritual and a metaphor for love. A happy relationship is about giving and receiving. If we can't find a compromise, we are over.'

Her last three words hit Tom in the stomach, as well as his solar plexus. He needed to buy some time. 'I guess I could try some fruit and – er – a few mushrooms now and again.'

'Is that a promise?'

Tom didn't understand her sudden mood swing, but he knew how to win. 'Of course it's a promise. As you said, "sharing meals is a metaphor for love" .'

Janet sat back down, she new exactly what she had to do. 'Well, if you're prepared to compromise, you'd better show me that engagement ring.'

Over the next few weeks, Tom stayed true to his word, trying most of the dishes she set before him, and as a member of the Animal Liberation Front, Janet was duty bound to liberate the lives of the hundreds of defenceless animals that would undoubtedly have passed through his lips.

Being a radical vegan demanded dedication and sacrifice, reasoned Janet, as she added a few more poisoned mushrooms to her fiancé's plate.

+++++

'Who Do You Think You Are?'

'I don't know what this area's coming to, Anne, I really don't. First it was sheep rustling, and now this.'

Nathan, just seven years old, stood before his parents, head bowed, staring at his sandals. He knew better than to speak before being spoken to.

His father repeated Nathan's story. 'So, let me get this straight. You were walking along, minding your own business, and these two men calmly walked up to you and stole our shopping.'

'Well, they didn't actually steal it, Dad, they just made it clear that their need was far greater than ours, so I handed it over, and they took it to their leader.'

'Well, I'm not standing for that. Stealing from a young boy indeed. Come on, let's go and find them.'

Father and son travelled along the dusty road until they reached the crowd who were gathered at the hillside. Followed closely by his father, Nathan weaved his way through the multitude until they reached the front.

'Right, son, point out this leader and I'll give him a piece of my mind.'

Nathan pointed. 'That's him, over there, the one with the beard, white robes and gold sandals.'

'Who do you think you are?' shouted Nathan's father, 'stealing our five loaves and two fish?'

Addiction

'Don't forget, I've got that meeting this afternoon and you promised you'd come with me.'

Tyler checked his phone. 'I promised my mum I'd tidy my bedroom but I haven't.'

'You're my best mate, Tyler, and I need your support. The meeting will only take an hour; you'll still have enough time left to get your fix.'

'Hey, I'm no addict.'

'Could you go a day without it?'

'Course I could, but I don't wanna, OK?'

'Methinks he doth protest too much.'

'Hey, you're the unhappy one, not me. I've got three girlfriends...'

'All cyber,' interrupted Ben.

'They're the best kind, mate, they can't boss you around.'

'Whatever.'

'OK, one hour; then I'm outta there. Are these meetings mixed?'

'Only you could see a meeting of addicts as a dating opportunity.'

'You were just telling me to get a proper girlfriend. Besides, you're not an addict, Ben; you only think you are.'

'I need to log-in first thing in the morning, during the day, and last thing at night.'

'So do most of your friends.'

'Mum says if I don't cut down, I'll go blind.'

'Why are you talking to the wall? I'm over here.'

'It's not funny, Tyler. I can't sleep, I can't relax, I'm not eating properly...'

'Enough already, I get the picture. I'll come with you.'

'And you promised to behave.'

'I can't believe I promised that... have I got time to log on for a quick session?'

'And you say you're not addicted?'

They reached the drab, depressing building nestled in an alleyway just off the High Street, and settled into two seats near the back of the hall, where at least 40 other people were present.

'Hey Ben, this room smells worse than your bedroom, mate.'

'Tyler, you promised.'

'OK, OK, yada yada.'

'Welcome everybody, my name's Dave and I think we should make a start. For our newcomers, please relax, you can sit quietly or give a testimony; it's entirely up to you. The first step to beating an addiction is to admit to yourself that you have a problem, so congratulations for taking that first step. In order to avoid distractions, please turn off your phones and gadgets. Now, who would like to start?'

Much to Ben's surprise, his best friend rose to his feet. 'Hello, my name is Tyler, I'm 16 years old, and I'm addicted to Facebook.'

Try Something New

Heaven could not be much better than this, thought Tommy Higgins, as he leaned into the early morning wind, his running shoes crunching leaves and twigs with every stride, his tracksuit clinging to his body as he reached the final turn. The early morning sun rose in the south, chasing away the early frost, the smell of damp woodland filled his senses and the trees, swaying in the wind, seemed to wave him goodbye as he reached the clearing, just short of the isolated cottage in which he hoped to begin his masterpiece.

Tommy was an author and a creature of habit. An early morning run, a shower and then a raw egg was his routine preparation before facing the blank, intimidating pages of his A4 notebook, not that he was short of ideas; he was in a rich grain of creativity including a new book to be called *Try Something New*. He hoped that it would help not only him, but others who were creatures of habit. Change was a good thing, he decided; it could stimulate new creativity and growth in a person.

Tommy left the woods in his wake and powered up the slight incline to the cottage, his sweat-covered eyes almost missing the container of eggs nestled in the grass verge. He skidded to a halt, took a breath, and retraced his steps. Three large eggs had been placed in a basket with a barely legible note: FREE EGGS. Who could have left them? There was no cottage for miles around, and nobody knew he was there, except for the anonymous online booking agent. Correction, he thought, gasping for breath, someone knew.

Tommy was a city boy, used to medium-sized brown eggs in a plastic egg box from the supermarket. 'Always check to see if any are cracked,' his mother taught him, 'It's no good finding out when you get home.' But these were not supermarket eggs, they were huge. Duck eggs perhaps, or pheasant eggs? Which game birds were common in Cornwall? He hadn't a clue. He picked up a large egg. Emus perhaps? These large eggs were not part of his routine. His routine food, including medium-sized brown supermarket eggs, lay on the kitchen floor in a box, waiting to be stored.

It would be rude to refuse this anonymous gift, he reasoned, and in any case, how could he write *Trying Something New* if he wasn't prepared to do so himself?

He chose the middle egg and lifted it head-high. The shell was a strange mottled brown and cream colour. 'Come on, eat your eggs, they're full of goodness and will make you strong,' his mother always told him.

His fingernails began to crack the shell; he tilted his head back as he lifted the egg over his mouth. For a second, the egg blotted out the morning sun, becoming almost transparent, and for a micro-second, the embryo inside seemed to move as he opened the shell and let the contents pour into his open mouth. The smell was putrid like mouldy cheese, and it took three almighty swallows for the contents to pass down his throat. He gagged violently like a celebrity in the Australian jungle, but Ant and Dec were nowhere to be seen.

He grabbed his water bottle, gulping down copious

amounts of water in an effort to remove the vile taste from his mouth. If that's what duck eggs taste like, you can keep 'em. His stomach did not take kindly to the invasion of foreign matter and all was not well with his insides.

He heard a strange howling noise from inside the woods, the sun dipped low behind distant clouds and the wind freshened as he carried the other large eggs into the kitchen of the cottage, placing them on the draining board.

Doubled up with pain, he staggered and fell onto the old settee. He suddenly wished that he was back in the comfort of his own home with Anna; at least she would know what to do.

Like the weather, his happiness deteriorated rapidly. He grabbed his notepad and sketched an outline of the morning's events, before lapsing into a long, haunted sleep.

He woke in unfamiliar surroundings, the dark clouds outside providing a gloomy atmosphere. The pains in his stomach quickly reminded him of his situation. He scanned the dusty interior of the old run-down cottage; the laughing cavalier picture over the open fireplace seemed to mock his predicament. He could barely move. He felt weak and in the grip of food poisoning or a stomach bug. In the shaft of light coming through the open kitchen door, he wrote a few more notes before lapsing unconscious.

The instant-replay of the moving embryo inside the eggshell caused him to wake with a start. Racked with stomach pains, he longed for his noisy children. Noise would be a good thing right now; it would take his mind off this nightmare situation.

He could feel his strength draining away minute-by-minute and his regular stomach pains were now accompanied by hot flushes. He would not make it to the front door, never mind his car, and the cottage, deliberately chosen for it's isolation, had no phone. Until this thing passed, he knew he was going nowhere, but he desperately needed water.

He lowered himself to the floor and inched across the room until the food box was within reach. His stomach seemed to grow with every pull, and pain intensified as he dragged the box back to the settee. Springs groaned once again, as he slumped back onto the settee. He slaked his thirst, the cold water cooling him a little. He grabbed his notepad and wrote down some more thoughts before lapsing into another horrific embroyo-moving nightmare.

Tommy woke in severe pain, gasping for breath. He removed his tracksuit top and T-shirt to combat the increasing hot flushes. This stomach bug was a nightmare of his own making. He had placed himself in the middle of nowhere to awaken his inner-self, and he had swallowed the raw egg. There was no one to blame but himself. He drank the last of his water; his stomach was huge now, and the water seemed to slosh around inside him, giving a sense of movement.

If only I wrote horror stories, he thought, this one would be a cracker. He pictured the scene from the film *Alien,* when a strange creature burst out of John Hurt's stomach. He stifled a laugh, causing another bout of pain. Am I going insane? He wrote down his thoughts before feeling around his ever-enlarging stomach. Was that a movement? Was that a kick?

His dreams were becoming more vivid and bizarre. How could a man possibly become pregnant, let alone with an alien's child? As he woke, the eerie silence was shattered by a large egg falling onto the kitchen floor. Purple liquid seeped out and as the crack widened, a scaly withered dead hand flopped into view, releasing the now familiar putrid smell. Tommy vomited over the side of the settee, purple and orange mucus stringing from his mouth. He grabbed his pen and scribbled, 'I have an alien growing inside me.'

Having just given birth to E.T. in another nightmare, he woke to find the room different somehow. Then he saw them; two hooded figures occupying the armchairs. A low, resonating, guttural voice whispered, 'Don't be alarmed, it's not good for you or junior.'

Instinctively, Tommy grabbed his stomach. There was definite movement inside. In the poorly lit room, he could not see the hooded figures clearly.

'Why me; why not a female jogger?'

'That's a good question but first, please take a drink, it will ease your pain.'

Tommy eyed the strange vessel beside him.

'I can assure you, it doesn't taste as bad as our placenta, go on, try something new.'

Tommy drank the luke warm liquid, his pain eased quickly and the thing inside him calmed down.

'You are thinking of birth only in human terms by the female of your species. Understandable, considering the situation.'

Tommy watched in horror as a thick red line slowly

zig-zagged down his chest and over his swollen stomach, as if drawn by an invisible marker, and the movement inside increased.

'You are *still* thinking in human terms and wondering how long to delivery. It won't be long now. Your nine-month gestation period is just one of the many failings of the human race. Please, take another drink.'

Needing more pain relief, Tommy did so. 'Human babies feed on nutrients from their mother, so what is junior feeding on?'

From the darkness beneath the hood, a strange voice replied: 'Just like a human baby will instinctively locate a nipple, so junior will have latched onto a blood vessel. Human blood has a lot going for it: temperature regulation, an immune system, the distribution of oxygen. Obviously the human body fails at everything else, like walking upright. Whose stupid idea was that? All that pressure on two feet, two ankles, two knees and two hips. But human blood, now that might prove to be the answer.'

'You mean I'm just an experiment?'

'On the contrary, think of yourself as a pioneer, and if your notes are good enough, you could become more famous than Doctor Christiaan Barnard, posthumously, of course. Please take another drink. Junior wants to come out and play.'

Tommy finished the last of the anaesthetic and watched in horror as the red jagged line down his body began to open. 'But how did you know that I'd eat the raw egg?'

'We put the thought in your head. I must

congratulate you on your swallowing technique.' The hooded figure then passed Tommy his notepad. 'Would you like to record your last thoughts?'

As Tommy scribbled his last words, his rib-cage cracked open. Purple juice came first, followed quickly by the now-familiar putrid smell as purple fingers emerged, tearing his flesh apart.

A low, resonating, guttural voice shouted louder and louder, 'It's a boy, it's a boy!'

Semi-conscious, and with tear-filled eyes, Tommy was paralysed with fear. Hands were shaking his shoulders and with the last of his strength, he fought desperately to shake them off.

'It's a boy, it's a boy,' said a deep melodic voice in a Welsh accent. *A Welsh accent?*

Tommy opened one eye. Shaking his shoulders was Nurse Bronwyn, and he was in the maternity hospital waiting room.

'It's a boy, Mr Higgins, and your wife and baby are doing fine. Would you like to see them now?'

+++++

'It was all a dream' is a criminal way to end a short story and I apologise.

The truth is that this actually happened to me! I did fall asleep in the waiting room, my wife did give birth to a boy, and every now and again, my son does behave like an alien.

Sign of the Times

Philip stared out of the window, his hands clasped behind his back. 'Are you going to be much longer?' His wife continued writing. 'I blame the Conservatives and what they did to the National Health Service.'

She put down her pen. 'That's typical of you, always wanting someone to blame. What about Labour? They made changes too?'

Philip turned and paced across the room to the other window. 'I was merely pointing out ...'

'Well, don't. Just let me get on with my work.' She picked up her pen and continued writing.

Philip shrugged his shoulders. 'Your mother never used to take this long.'

'Yes, but that was another time and place.'

'No it wasn't, it was right here in this room. She sat on that same chair at the same desk, and probably used the very same pen. Couldn't you ask one of our servants to help you?'

'Wouldn't that be forgery? It's my job and only I can do it. Would you really like to help me?'

'Anything, my dear; after all, I am one of your servants. What would you like me to do?'

'Take the dogs for a walk. I'll have one of the servants find you when I'm finished.'

As he left the room, the Queen picked up her pen and continued signing telegrams for her 100-year-old subjects.

A
Royal Wedding
in Somerset

William sat on the throne, trying to remember details of his night out with Harry. His fiancée Kate shouted up the stairs, 'Breakfast is on the table.' She knew that William hated it when she shouted up the stairs.

After a late-night session with his brother, breakfast for William was usually two choices: take it or leave it, but this morning, his fiancée had made a special effort. He came downstairs to find a full English breakfast of bacon, sausages, mushrooms, eggs and tomatoes, with fried bread on the side. He absently scratched his crown jewels and yawned. 'Morning, Kate; breakfast looks fit for a king.'

Sitting down to her customary two boiled eggs, a slim-line Kate avoided eye contact. 'Morning, Willie.' She always called him 'Willie' when he was in her bad books, and William was fully aware of this.

'"Morning Willie" is how someone might address their manhood first thing in the morning, hardly the correct way to address a member of the Royal family.'

'Excuse me, your majesty, but who died and made you king? There's no need to get above your station.' The use of clichés and puns was deliberate because William hated them.

'I don't get above my station – do I?'

'No, your majesty,' replied Kate, smashing the shell of an egg with her spoon. 'So what did you and Harry get up to last night? Come on, spill the beans.' She decided to squeeze in as many clichés as she could.

Beans! William knew there was something wrong with breakfast. No baked beans. What's going on? He had tomatoes instead of beans. Does she think I'm getting fat? He ate another mouthful of food. 'Kate, do you think I'm getting fat?'

Kate looked him over. 'You know what they say; a minute on the lips, a lifetime on the hips. It wouldn't hurt you to get into shape for the wedding photographs.' That would teach him for staying out late with his brother.

'I'm round. That's a shape, isn't it? It's not like I haven't tried to lose weight; it's just that one's body and one's fat have become real good friends.'

Kate cracked her second boiled egg as if to say, *this is what you should be eating – healthy food, not fried bacon and sausage,* then she asked again about last night. 'Did you go clubbing?'

A silly grin spread across William's face. 'Don't be silly, Kate, there are no seals in Weston-super-Mare.'

Kate ignored him. He was always childish after a night out with Harry. 'He never takes life seriously, does he?'

'Who, the laughing policeman?'

'You know full well who I mean, your brother Harry. He gets right up my nose.'

'That reminds me of one of Harry's jokes: "Why do gorillas have big nostrils?"' He could see from the look on her face that she would not answer, so in a poor attempt at a female voice, he answered his own question. '"I don't know, Harry; why do gorillas have big nostrils?" "Because they have big fingers!"' William laughed aloud at his joke-telling skills.

Seeing that Kate was not impressed, William tried to be serious.

'Last night, Harry suggested that we should both return to Africa to give more support to that AIDS charity we helped a few years ago.'

'Is that before our wedding, or afterwards?'

'Kate, will you please go easy on Harry? After our marriage he will be left all on his own, and right now, he just doesn't know who he is anymore. He feels a bit like that guy from Wham! when George Michael left.'

'What guy?'

'Exactly!'

Kate steered the conversation back to the wedding. 'William, we still have important decisions to make; for instance, what will you do with your corgis once we are married?' William was straight on the defensive. 'I'm not getting rid of them; they have brought me untold pleasure for many years.'

'Can't Harry look after them for you?'

'You must be joking. Harry can't look after himself, never mind my corgis. They need care and attention. I'll have you know, some of them are nearly 40 years old.'

'And they look it too,' sighed Kate. On more than one occasion, she had sat on one left on the settee, or found one in their bed.

William removed one of his corgis from his trouser

pocket. 'I admit that some of my corgis do need a lick of paint, like this light blue miniature Ford Anglia police car.' He held it before his eyes, studying it like a jeweller assessing an exquisite diamond.

'Little things please little minds,' said Kate, wishing that he would see her as an object of desire. She felt better for getting the Corgi problem out in the open. All's fair in love and war. Goodness, she thought, I'm even thinking in clichés now.

William decided to divert the conversation *back* to the wedding, a grave misjudgement.

'I thought you were happy with our fairytale royal wedding in Somerset? The abbey is booked, and many girls dream of walking down the aisle in an abbey.'

'Ah, yes, the ruins of Glastonbury Abbey: every young girl's dream wedding venue.'

'Well, it may not be too late to book Weston-super-Mare Grand Pier. Do you want me to phone them?'

'Oh, be still my beating heart! Weston's Grand Pier, every young girl's second dream wedding venue.'

'And don't forget, I've booked the castle for the evening reception.'

'Ah yes, the castle at Banwell, and we all know what parking is like at Banwell Castle. These wedding arrangements are hardly the red carpet treatment, are they? William, it's as plain as the nose on your face, we are not singing from the same hymn sheet.'

Much to Kate's annoyance, William took another Corgi out of his pocket, and began to use sound effects as he moved the two of them around the kitchen table, replicating a car chase. 'Brrrrrumm, yeeeeoooow, da da da da,' he sang, weaving the cars between the salt and pepper containers.

That was the straw that broke the camel's back. He was asking for it, and come hell or high water, he was going to get it, right between the eyes. She took a deep breath and decided to hit him with both barrels; after all, you always hurt the one you love.

'William, I know you think that you are a diamond geezer, but at the end of the day, with all due respect, when all is said and done, we have to face the facts, *Willie.*'

She put so much emphasis on the word 'Willie', William stopped the car chase and looked up.

'There's no point in beating around the bush; I can safely say, without fear of contradiction, that you are all icing and no cake. In fact, the only thing regal about you, William Royal – is your surname!'

+++++

Colourful Argument

Roses are red, Edna, violets are blue,
a face like yours belongs in a zoo.
Oh, don't feel sad, Clive, don't feel blue,
Frankenstein was ugly too.

Your skin is wrinkled Edna, your hair ghostly white,
in the light of the moon, you do look a fright.
Hark who's talking Clive, you're bald with a tan,
a poor excuse for a gentleman.

Your teeth are false Edna, your nails are black,
I think it's time I gave you the sack.
Snow is white Clive, pansies are violet,
who will you find to put you on the toilet?

Someone with warm hands Edna, that's for sure,
on your way out, please close the green door.
Clive, you need me to feed you peaches and apricot,
who will you find to empty your pot?

You're old and grey, Clive, and as slow as a tortoise,
that's shut you up, have you lost your voice?
Clive, you don't usually take this long,
have I won again? Cat got your tongue?

It's baiting me that keeps you alive,
what do you say to that, Clive. Clive?Clive?

Dressed to Kill

On Saturday nights when she was drunk, Gemma made bad decisions, like flashing her breasts, mooning passing motorists, or running naked along Weston-super-Mare seafront.

After four cocktails and three tequila slammers, her latest bet with Chloe was relatively tame. Finding the right man to do it with, now that could be difficult. What she needed was a loner.

Gemma ran out of the nightclub, straight into the arms of a man dressed like a vampire.

'You are just what the doctor ordered,' she gasped in amazement.

'No, I think you'll find that Frankenstein's monster was created by a doctor. I'm a vampire and I suck people's blood.'

She pulled her blonde hair to one side and tilted her head, exposing her neck. 'You're perfect then, please bite me just there.'

As other revellers in fancy dress passed them by, the vampire's eyes glowed brightly in the moonlight. 'But shouldn't we go on a date first, or hold hands, or go through some sort of courting ritual? At the very least, shouldn't we exchange names?'

'OK, Count whatever your name is, nice make-up by the way, very realistic – not! I'm Gemma Watson, and my friend Chloe has bet me £5 that she will get a love-bite from a stranger first. There's no time to lose. Please, bite my neck; then I can send her the picture by mobile phone and I'll be the winner.'

'Well, if you put it like that, how can I refuse? Your wish is my command, but not here; let's go down by the side of the pier.'

His request for a secluded spot did not raise any alarm bells to an inebriated Gemma. Her only focus was on winning the bet.

In the shadows of Weston-super-Mare Grand Pier, the vampire gave Gemma the love-bite she so desired. His fangs pierced her jugular vein as he drank the elixir of life.

After dragging her lifeless corpse under the pier, he picked up her mobile phone, searched through the contacts list, and made a call.

'Hello, is that Chloe? I've just bumped into Gemma and she told me about your crazy £5 bet. How would you like to be the winner? If you come and meet me by the pier, I can help you.'

'Great,' she said. 'I'm just across the road. How will I recognise you?'

'That's easy; I'm dressed like a vampire.'

+++++

First Impressions

Glen Smith was strong and well-built due to his love of the gym, but his girlfriend Candice reduced him to a shivering wreck with words that struck fear into his heart. 'It's time to meet my parents.'

Damn, bugger and blast, thought Glen, the stress of her words inducing one of his panic attacks. 'When?'

'This Saturday, at 6pm.'

Crikey, flipping heck. 'That's a bit short notice?'

'Mum's a great cook. You're not a vegan, are you?'

'No, I'm definitely human, and I'm quite partial to a slice of dead cow, as it happens.' Humour was Glen's best defence to keep his nerves in check.

'There's nothing to worry about, as long as you follow the house rules.'

Damn, bugger and blast. 'Just how many rules are there?'

'My parents are house-proud, so it goes without saying that you should compliment them on the decor.'

'Goes without saying.' *Flipping heck, I know as much about interior decorating as Adolf Hitler.*

'And etiquette is important, table manners, that sort of thing.'

'No problems.' On the surface he remained calm, but under the surface...

Donald Fothergill dragged himself home from another boring week at the bank, looking forward to a cold beer; but his wife Audrey had other ideas.

'I've invited Candice and her boyfriend around for a meal tomorrow.'

'Tomorrow? But I'm half-way through finishing the upstairs bathroom. You'll have to re-arrange.'

Audrey Fothergill had never re-arranged in her life. 'No, my dear, you will have to work faster. Glen and Candice will be arriving here at 6.30pm and dinner will be served at 7pm precisely. I expect your presence, and a working upstairs toilet. Do I make myself clear? Of course, if you can't manage, our new neighbour Terry is a plumber. The blond chap, you must have seen him, he has muscles in all the right places. Should I give him a call?'

Although he was only five years older than Audrey, Donald's greatest fear was that she would leave him for a younger man. No way would a young muscular plumber be setting foot in their house. 'I'm quite capable of finishing in time, thank you very much.' The real reason that he took his time was, well, Audrey had become more and more demanding lately, in the you-know-what department.

'What do we know about this boyfriend, anyway? She's brought some right drips home, these last few years.'

'Audrey, really! Let's give the poor boy a chance.'

As an only child, Candice was used to getting her own way, and liked everything to be just so. As she checked her hair and make-up in her mirror, she spoke to Glen. '...do not burp or pass wind...' *Damn, bugger and blast.* '...do not pick your nose, or scratch any part of your anatomy.'

Damn, bugger and blast. 'Will I be allowed to breathe?'

'Yes, but not heavily, I don't want mother to get the wrong impression, and Glen, get rid of that chewing gum.'

Damn, bugger and blast. He pretended to swallow it, but continued chewing slowly and discretely. His second line of defence was chewing gum.

'And don't say you're a barman, say bar manager or steward...' *Damn, bugger and blast.* Glen's secret chewing went into overdrive, '...and NO jokes! Mother doesn't enjoy jokes.'

Glen gripped the steering wheel; his knuckles and his face were white. This was going to be a long night.

On seeing Glen's broad shoulders, Audrey wished that she was 20 years younger. 'Good evening, Glen, please come in. 'May I take your coat?'

Damn, bugger and blast. Glen worried about sweat stains under his arms. 'No, if it's all the same to you, Mrs Fothergill...'

'Please, call me Audrey. Would you like a drink?'

'Yes please.' *Just what the doctor ordered, a cold beer.* His chewing slowed down.

'Tea or coffee?' said Audrey.

Glen's chewing increased.

'He drinks coffee, as-a-rule,' said Candice.

As-a-rule? Oh, yes, the rules. Glen, pulled himself together, 'Audrey, I do love the flowery wallpaper in this room, it's really, really rather...'

'Rather ghastly and I detest it, and if Donald ever finishes the upstairs bathroom, removing that hideous pink wallpaper will be his next job. Please excuse me whilst I go and make the drinks.' On her way to the kitchen, Audrey paused at the foot of the stairs. 'Donald,' she screeched, tarnishing her posh veneer, 'our guests are here. Can we have the pleasure of your company, sooner, rather than later?'

'That went well,' said Glen, hopefully.

Donald had been connecting the toilet waste when Audrey called. He raised his head to answer, cracking his skull on the cistern, 'Coming, dear.' He reached the bottom of the stairs just in time for coffee. 'So, Glen, is our daughter your first girlfriend?'

Damn, bugger, and blast, the interrogation has started already. 'Before Candice, I almost had a psychic girlfriend.'

'Almost?' said Audrey.

'Yes, but she left me before we met.' Silence confirmed his worst fears. His best form of defence, his sense of humour, was clearly not working.

'Daddy works at the bank and mummy's a secretary,' said Candice proudly.

Rules, Glen, remember the rules. 'I'm a bar steward.'

'I beg your pardon?' said Audrey.

'I work behind a bar serving beer.'

Donald decided to come to Glen's rescue. 'I work behind a counter too. Have you ever served anyone important?'

Glen began to relax, a non-threatening strand of conversation at last. 'Funny you should ask,' he began, receiving a stamp on his toes from Candice. 'Charles

Dickens came into the bar last night and ordered a martini. I said, "Olive or twist?"'

Much to Audrey's annoyance, Donald not only laughed, he went to the kitchen and returned with two cold beers. 'Here, Glen, you look like you could do with one of these.'

'Donald! Shut up and act your age!'

'Act my age? I've never been my age before, I have no experience.'

Audrey stormed into the kitchen, closely followed by Candice.

'Mum, can't you do something? Can't you make Dad behave like he promised?'

Audrey tasted the curry. 'Boys will be boys, dear, you'll just have to get used to it. Please tell them the food's ready, I'm about to dish up.'

Back in the living room, two kindred spirits swopped jokes over a beer. 'I go to a woman dentist,' said Donald. 'It's a nice change to be told by a female to open my mouth, not shut it.'

'Quasimodo came into my bar last night and ordered a whisky. I said, "How's the Bells?" and he said, "Don't you start!"'

The relaxed atmosphere ended when they were summoned to the dining table and Glen clapped eyes on a large pot of curry in pride of place. *Damn, bugger and blast.* Glen's chewing went into overdrive, prompting Candice to signal for him to lose it.

In a well-practised manoeuvre, Glen raised his napkin to his mouth, pinched his gum into the corner, and quickly lowered the napkin to the table.

Unfortunately some gum caught in his teeth and strings of gum clung to his clothes. *Damn, bugger and blast.* The more he wiped with the napkin, the more the gum and napkin spread. Donald brought a cloth from the kitchen and valiantly tried to help clean up the mess.

Audrey was quickly losing patience. 'If you two have quite finished, would it be possible for us to eat, whilst the curry is still hot?' She turned to Glen, pointing at the bowl of curry, 'After you.'

'Thank you, Audrey,' he said through clenched teeth. 'It looks lovely.' Hot spicy food did not agree with Glen. He put a small amount on his plate and smothered it in rice. Eventually, everyone was ready to eat. Under close scrutiny, Glen raised curry to his lips, praying for it to be mild. As he started to choke and splutter, particles of curry added to the mess on his jacket.

'Audrey does make a good vindaloo,' said Donald.

Glen needed the loo, and water, for his burning throat. He jumped up. 'Can I use your bathroom?'

'It's at the top of the stairs, first door on the right. You can be the guest of honour, but don't touch the wall tiles; I've only just grouted them.'

In the bathroom, cold water eased the burning in Glen's throat, but the curry had upset his constitution, leaving him no alternative but to use the toilet. Having spotted a can of air freshener, he relaxed, and did what he had to do. He looked for some toilet paper. *Damn, bugger and blast.* No toilet paper!

In the dining room, Candice was upset. 'Dad, you promised me you would be on your best behaviour.'

'Candice, love, it's hardly fair on the young man, is it, especially one so nervous.'

Candice stormed up to her bedroom in a strop and flung herself on her bed.

Audrey ate some more curry. 'Do you think Candice is spoilt?'

'Does Elton John wear a wig? Of course she's spoilt, but at least, this time, she's brought back a decent down-to-earth human being. I, for one, am not going to put on airs and graces any longer. I think I'm going to like Glen.'

'Talking of Glen, that boy's been an awfully long time upstairs?'

Candice had stopped sulking, touched up her make-up and, on leaving her bedroom, found her father outside the bathroom door.

'Glen, are you in there? Is everything all right?'

Donald put his arm around his daughter. 'On first impressions, as long as Glen respects you and our house, I think he'll be just fine.'

In the bathroom, Glen had used his Y-fronts to clean himself, but when he tried to flush them away, they blocked the toilet, and the harder he rammed the brush down the toilet, the more the water overflowed.

Glen stood back in horror as the puddle of water edged nearer and nearer the bathroom door. *Damn, bugger and blast.*

50-WORD MINI-SAGAS

Driving Tip

Avoid getting yourself prosecuted for using your mobile phone while driving. Hide it inside a large seashell and police will think you're listening to the ocean. As far as I am aware, nobody has been prosecuted for listening to a seashell.

Better still, why not buy yourself a hands-free kit?

Who is the Smartest?

'They say a roomful of monkeys with typewriters will eventually produce the entire works of Shakespeare, gibbon half a chance.'

'Listen, dolphins are the smartest of animals. Within a few weeks of captivity, they can train people to stand on the edge of a pool and throw fish to them.'

Too Much Information

'They say that if you have a blockage you should try something different, so last night, on my way home, I had a curry and a pint, and it worked. I really flowed this morning and filled three sheets.'

'Too much information, dear, but I'm glad you're enjoying writers' group.'

A Friend in Need
is a Friend Indeed

Jane topped up their wine glasses for the third time as they helped each other through recent relationship break-ups. 'I think all the decent men are gone.'

'And the indecent men,' laughed Angelica.

They clinked wine glasses.

'So, Jane, how come you and Tony split up? I thought you were a match made in heaven?'

'I wanted a threesome.'

'And he didn't?'

'He was the wrong sex.'

'Oh, Jane, what are you like!' They clinked glasses again.

Jane loved entertaining in her penthouse apartment.

'So tell me, Angelica, what happened with you and Ted? I thought you two were good together?'

Angelica puffed out her cheeks. 'He was too in touch with his feminine side.'

'Isn't that a good thing?'

'Not in his case.'

'Tell me more. Did he start cooking, doing housework and faking orgasms?'

They both laughed, clinked their glasses and drank more wine.

'No. I came home early from work and caught him wearing my knickers. It wouldn't have been so bad, but he looked better in them than I do.'

'I doubt that,' said Jane, quickly adding, 'not with

his beer-belly.' She topped up their wine glasses.

Despite Angelica's bravado, helped along by a few glasses of wine, it was obvious to Jane that her friend was still hurting from her break-up with Ted. Jane put down her wine glass and opened her arms. 'I hate seeing you upset like this. Come here, you look like you need a hug.'

Angelica melted into her friend's arms and her tears began to flow.

Jane stroked her friend's dark hair for a few minutes before reaching for the tissues. 'Let it all out my angel, it's OK. Remember, I'm always here for you when you need a shoulder to cry on. Here, dry your eyes.'

Angelica, the shorter of the two, looked up at Jane through tear-stained eyes. 'You must think I'm really weak, going to pieces like this. I'm sorry for getting all soppy and emotional.'

'Don't be sorry, my angel, that's what I love about you.'

Angelica looked deep into Jane's hazel eyes. 'Did you just say, "...that's what I love about you"?'

+++++

Born to be Wild

It was the third week in July 1969, and many factories had closed for the annual holidays. Stuck in heavy traffic, Mr Ford strummed his fingers against the steering wheel of his Ford Cortina. Behind him, his twin daughters flicked through pop magazines. Sixteen-year-old Alice pointed at song lyrics and began to sing, *she loves you, yeah, yeah, yeah, she loves you, yeah, yeah, yeah, yeah.* Roxy, her sister, covered her ears.

One hour later, Mrs Ford pointed through the windscreen. 'There it is, girls, can you see the flags? Butlins holiday camp.'

After the family had checked in at reception, a 'barrow-boy' wearing the name badge 'Roger' loaded their suitcases onto his trolley and led them through rows of identical red chalets. Trailing behind were twins Roxy and Alice.

'What about him?' said Roxy. 'You've got to lose your cherry some day, and he looks mighty strong.'

Alice ignored her.

'Do you want me to fix you up?' Roxy continued.

Alice blushed as red as the chalets. 'Don't you dare!'

Roger winked at Alice before leaving the family of four outside chalet 27 in Yellow Camp.

Mrs Ford opened her purse, pulling out two half-crowns. 'Now, girls, what do you do if you get lost?'

'Ask a redcoat,' they shouted, grabbing the coins and heading off to explore. As they passed the swimming pool, Roxy pointed at a muscular lifeguard.

'What about him?'

'Just because you're five minutes older than me, Roxy, that doesn't give you the right to organise my love life.'

'Love? Who said anything about love? It's the swinging sixties and it's time you joined in. It would help if you did something with your hair...'

'I prefer short hair, like Twiggy.'

As they argued, Roger passed them by, pushing more suitcases on his trolley. He smiled again at Alice. Blushing deeply, Alice turned to her sister. 'Don't say a word.'

One hour later, they joined over 2,000 people in York dining hall. Tables and chairs were numbered and set in long rows on a red, yellow and blue tiled floor, and dinner was run with military precision.

'OK, girls, some rules,' explained their father: 'you get one key between you, and as long as you promise to behave yerselves and stick together, you don't have to stay with us 24 hours a day, but if you don't...'

'We promise,' shouted the twins, both grabbing for the key. Roxy held the key triumphantly. 'Can we go and explore the camp?'

'OK, but be back by 6pm; it's Welcome Night in the main ballroom.'

'Are you sure that's wise?' asked his wife, as their daughters disappeared from sight.

'What, takin' 'em to the welcome night?'

'Giving them so much freedom. This *is* their first real holiday, after all.'

'It's *my* first real holiday an' all. Forty-eight weeks each year, I work in that factory. A bit o' peace and quiet wouldn't go amiss. Those redcoats will keep an eye on 'em. Anyroad, shouldn't you 'ave a word to Roxy about her short skirts?

'It's the fashion, dear.'

The Beachcomber Bar, with a totem pole entrance and bamboo roof, was just down the hill from Yellow Camp. 'Come on, Alice, let's check it out.'

'Just arrived, girls?' asked the waiter. 'May I recommend the knickerbocker glory? It's only three-and-sixpence, and it contains three kinds of ice cream, plus fruit, raspberry sauce, a wafer and a cherry.'

'If someone don't want their cherry, would you remove it for them?' asked Roxy, receiving a kick from her sister. The puzzled barman offered his hand.

'I'm Alex. Find yourselves a seat, and I'll bring them over.' He served their ice creams a few minutes later. 'These are on the house; maybe I'll see you later at the welcome night?'

In the Gaiety Theatre, they found an empty table and four chairs, and Mr Ford joined the queue at the bar.

'Can we go to the arcade?' pleaded Roxy. 'This welcome thing is gonna be so-o-o boring.'

Mrs Ford opened her purse. 'Here's ten bob each; you stick together – and be back in one hour.'

At the bar, Mr Ford downed a pint of hand-pulled mild and returned to the table with his second pint, half a lager and two Cresta lemonades. 'Where are they?'

'Gone to the amusement arcade for an hour.'

'Are you sure that's wise?' he said, sarcastically.

Roxy led the way to the bright lights and loud music of the dodgems, and when she climbed into a car, her mini-skirt caused a stir.

'Hi, my name's Spike,' said the long-haired attendant, hopping onto the back of her car.

'I'm Roxy.'

To the sound of Chuck Berry, Spike jumped from car to car collecting the last of the fares, as cars began moving. Alice deliberately rammed Roxy's car a few times, payback for her constant teasing.

After an hour, Alice, the more sensible of the two, tugged Roxy's arm and pointed at her watch. 'Come on, let's not upset our folks on the first night.'

It was past midnight when a drunken Mr Ford led the family back to their chalet. Roxy whispered to Alice. 'If we play our cards right, this week could be wild.'

'No it won't. You'll find a way to screw things up; you always do.'

Sunday was spent on the beach, located beyond a gate at the rear of the camp and accessed by a long walk or chairlift. The twins climbed into the first two-seater chairlift car, their parents into the next, and when all were full, the cars began moving faster and faster over the camp below.

Alice leaned to one side. 'Look, there's Yellow Camp, there's Red Camp, and those chalets with no colour must be the staff chalets, and look, there's Roger.' She leaned out the side, waving frantically.

Roxy gripped her seat with white knuckles. 'Keep bloody still, will ya?'

The twins were well behaved at the beach; they didn't want to miss the evening disco.

The Regency Disco consisted of rotating coloured lights on top of two giant speakers, between which were two record decks and a partly hidden DJ. Coloured lights swept the dance floor, occasionally picking out fluorescent pictures on jet black walls. Alice, wearing a T-shirt, Levi's and trainers, was soon dancing, but after watching campers do the Twist and the Shadows' walk, leather-clad Roxy climbed onto the stage.

'Have you got any decent records?'

The DJ pointed over his shoulder. 'Check out the back room.'

Roxy entered, to find a mattress, a table, and cans of cider, but no records. She opened a can and took a swig. After starting another record, the DJ joined her and stole a kiss. 'Welcome to Bruno's love shack.'

'Confident, aren't ya?' said Roxy, pushing him away. 'Play *Born to Be Wild* for me, and it just might be your lucky night.'

Returning to the crowded dance floor, Roxy found Alice. 'Fancy losing your cherry tonight? Bruno, the DJ, has a love shack *and* cider at the back of the stage. Go check him out, and I'll keep a lookout for Mum.'

Alice pulled a packet of mints from her pocket. 'Have one of these; if you breathe cider on Mum, the holiday will be over before it's begun.'

In the Empire Theatre, thousands of campers watched on screen as the lunar shuttle landed on the moon.

'You stay here and drink your beer, love; I'll go and check on the girls.'

At the sight of her mum entering the disco, Roxy climbed on stage and crept into the love shack, where Alice and Bruno jumped apart. 'We're in big trouble; Mum's outside looking for us.'

'Don't panic,' said Bruno. 'What's she wearing?'

'A blue polka-dot dress and white shoes.'

Bruno returned to the stage, started another record, and watched her. A few minutes later, he returned to the love shack. 'Quick, she's gone into the toilets.'

Mrs Ford hurried from the toilets, to find the twins on the dance floor. 'Where have you been?'

'We got hot from dancing,' said Roxy, sucking hard on a mint, 'so we nipped out for some fresh air.'

'Well, I've come to fetch you; someone's about to step on the moon.'

To the sound of *Born to Be Wild*, the twins reluctantly left the dancefloor with their mother.

On the boating lake the next day, Roxy explained her scoring system to Alice. 'In my diary, I write their names and award marks out of 10. Last night, I gave Bruno an 8 for kissing, and he's pretty good with his hands.'

'Please, spare me the sordid details, Roxy, and try using that paddle; going round in circles is making me feel sick.'

In the afternoon, as they sunbathed by the swimming pool, Roxy whispered to Alice, 'How close were you to losing your cherry with Bruno last night?'

Alice could not understand her sister's need to boast about liaisons with the opposite sex.

In the snooker hall, Spike and Bruno discussed the twins. 'One can of cider and that Roxy's anybody's, if you ask me.'

'What about her twin, Alice?'

'Nah, Roxy's the one. I bet you £5, I sleep with her first.'

'OK, shake on it.'

That evening, whilst their parents enjoyed more drinks in the Gaiety Theatre, the twins spent more time flirting with boys at the amusement arcade. Spike and Bruno both invited Roxy to their staff chalets. 'The amusements are closed daily, 1pm to 2pm; why not come and join us?' Bruno offered cider, and, not to be outdone, Spike offered marijuana. In reply, Roxy invited them to the cinema on Wednesday evening to watch *Easy Rider.*

In the darkness of the cinema, Roxy did not see much of the film, she was too busy snogging Spike and Bruno alternately. When it wasn't his turn, Spike shared a joint with Alice, but when he tried to snog her, she pushed him away.

Alice was not used to smoking pot, and told Roxy she could see large pink rabbits smoking joints and riding Harley-Davidsons, so when they rejoined their parents in the Gaiety Theatre, Roxy, sucking heavily on a mint, tried in vain to cover their tracks. 'People behind us were smoking pot, Mum, and it's made Alice feel ill.'

'That rabbit's staring at me,' said Alice, looking at the empty stage, 'make him stop.' Then she threw up.

Despite Roxy pleading their innocence, Mr Ford was having none of it. 'You're both grounded.'

Wednesday was another family day at the beach, but around mid-day, Alice asked if she could return to the chalet because she felt ill.

'You do look a bit pale, Alice. Roxy, go with her and keep an eye on her.'

'I'll be OK, Mum, honest. I just need a lie down.'

Key in hand, Alice left the others at the beach and

caught the chairlift back to camp.

Half an hour later, Roxy volunteered to go check on Alice, but when she reached the chalet, there was no answer. Must be asleep, thought Roxy, heading for the amusement arcade.

Spike was waiting. 'Fancy coming to my chalet?'

'I can't. Alice had a bad trip yesterday and we're both grounded. Have you seen her today?' Spike shook his head and sloped off.

Roxy returned to the chalet, to find Alice inside. 'Where have you been? I knocked earlier.'

Alice yawned. 'I must have been asleep.'

During dinner on Thursday, fate played a hand. The champagne spinner stopped on chalet number 27, and then row 56, and redcoats delivered a large bottle of champagne to the table of the Ford family.

'I've never won anything before,' giggled Mrs Ford, as she and her husband finished off the champagne in their chalet.

Mr Ford could see a twinkle in his wife's eye, and needed the twins out of the chalet. He offered the spare key to Roxy. 'Go on, get yerselves down to the amusements for an hour.'

Roxy read the situation and decided to push for more. 'And can we go to the disco tonight?'

He turned to his wife, who nodded.

Eating knickerbocker glory in the Beachcomber Bar, Roxy decided: 'Tonight, I'm gonna visit Bruno in the love shack; what about you? Isn't it time you lost this?' She grabbed the cherry off the top of Alice's ice cream and threw it away.

'Maybe I will,' said Alice, 'if only to stop your

teasing.'

'I think Mum will check up on us every hour, so the safest time to visit the love shack will be straight after she leaves. Do you wanna go first, or second?'

'You can go first,' said Alice.

Back in the chalet, Alice abandoned her Levi jeans for a knee-length denim skirt.

'Good thinking, sis,' said Roxy, who was wearing her usual black leather mini-skirt. 'After tonight, I do believe my teasing will have to stop.'

The disco started and Roxy climbed on stage to tell Bruno the plan. 'Mum will be checking on us every hour, so as soon as she leaves, we'll both take a turn in the love shack; it's your lucky night.'

Bruno rubbed the back of her thigh. 'I can't wait. Listen; to get you in the mood, I've hidden two cans of cider behind the curtain to the left of the stage.'

Mr and Mrs Ford supped their drinks and listened to the big band sound in the Gaiety Theatre. 'I've not seen Alice like that before,' said Mr Ford. 'Pink rabbits indeed. I'd expect Roxy to pull a stunt, but not Alice. Maybe we've given 'em too much freedom?'

'They won't get up to any mischief tonight, don't you fret. I'll check up on 'em every half-hour. In fact, I think I'll pay them a surprise visit right now. You relax and enjoy your beer, you've earned it.'

Between dances, both Roxy and Alice calmed their nerves with drinks of cider, always on the lookout for Mum, who almost caught them by surprise with her first visit. Conscious of cider on her breath, Alice simply said, 'Dance?' and grabbed her mum's hands.

'What, to this racket? No thank you. Now you girls behave yourselves, you hear?'

Both twins held in their cider breath, gave the thumbs up, and watched her until she had left the room.

Bruno played *Born to Be Wild*, and Roxy joined him in the love shack. They kissed, and he gave her more cider. 'I'm just gonna put on *Hey Jude*.'

'But I hate the Beatles.'

He smacked her backside. 'So do I, but this record's seven minutes long.'

Seven minutes later, after re-arranging her clothes, Roxy returned to the dance floor.

'How was he?' asked Alice.

'Eight out of ten, and he's really looking forward to taking your cherry.'

They saw Mum coming and were both sucking mints by the time she reached them.

'Dad wants you to rejoin us. Come on. He says you've had enough time on your own.'

'But the DJ is about to play Alice *Cherry Cherry* by Neil Diamond. Can we have 15 more minutes, please?'

'OK, but no more. I mean it.'

As soon as her mum left the disco, Alice joined Bruno in the love shack, and a short while later she rejoined Roxy on the dance floor.

'So how was it?'

'OK, I suppose, but I really don't know what all the fuss is about.'

'It should be better second time, when you're more relaxed,' said Roxy.

On Friday morning, with the bet won, Spike paid Bruno

his £5 and they gave the twins a wide berth. During the afternoon, as Mrs Ford packed so that they could leave on Friday evening to miss the Saturday traffic, the twins passed the time by filling in their diaries.

Roxy wrote: *Bruno, 5 out of 10.* She had a tear in her eye as she slammed her diary shut. After years of anticipation, she had always imagined that losing her cherry would be really special, but it wasn't. Bruno was rough, selfish and uncaring. She fought back tears of disappointment. Why didn't I keep up the pretence for longer, and wait for Mr Right to come along?

Alice wrote: *Bruno 0 out of 10,* and smiled. Roxy will stop teasing me now, and she'll never know that I didn't let him. Besides, he wasn't my type.

As Mr Ford drove towards the exit, Roger the barrow-boy blew Alice a kiss and waved her goodbye. Alice discreetly waved back and blew a kiss in return.

Roger had been just her type. Not only had his staff chalet been easy to find on Wednesday during her feigned illness; he had also proved to be a considerate and caring lover. A definite 10 out of 10.

+++++

ONE-ACT PLAY: MONOLOGUE

Over My Dead Body

You're going back to your mother's? Over my dead body! Anyway, you can't leave now, your broomstick's in for a service.

What do you mean, you've had enough? I know life can be frustrating, dear, but one day, trust me, you *will* find a hair stylist that you like.

What's brought this on, anyway?

I talk down to you? Well of course I do, I'm 6ft tall and you're 5ft small.

How long have you felt this way?

How long is a piece of string?

I think you'll find that How Long plays football for Manchester United, and his brother, How's That, plays cricket for Somerset.

My verbal diarrhoea's mental torture? Ha, ha, ha, ha. This mental torture thing; it's all in your mind.

Your snoring's like mental torture. I'd rather listen to Rolf Harris play his didgeridoo than listen to your snoring.

Your friends have told you to divorce me? But you only have three friends, and two of them are imaginary. On what grounds would you divorce me? Do I beat you? Have I been unfaithful? You'll be laughed out of the divorce courts.

(turns to left) Madam, on what grounds do you divorce this man?
(turns to right) Well, m'lud, he always has to have the last word.
(turns to left) So?

(SILENCE)

I must say, I do like a good argument.

It's Agnes who's put you up to this, isn't it? Good old Agnes. It wasn't that long ago she was trying to get into my pants, and there's not room for two of us, I can tell you.

Where did you get those handcuffs? That's an interesting twist, my dear. Wish I'd thought of that. Do you want me to undress first, or just put them on?

OK, I'll put them on. This is exciting. There, now I'm at your mercy. *(moves in front of her)* But you still can't leave. Our marriage vows are quite clear: till death us do part. *(checks pulse)* And I'm still very much alive.

(expression changes from excitement to concern)

W-w-where did you get that from? *(steps back)* that gun? May I remind you, the plan was to argue, then kiss and passionately make up? I know some days, it's hardly worth chewing through the restraining straps, dear, but isn't this taking things a bit far?

That wasn't your plan? So these handcuffs are to render me helpless? YOU CONNIVING BITCH!

OK, OK. I'll get down on my knees. *(sinks to knees)*

Listen, I know you say that I don't listen to a word you say - or something like that – but I can change.

Don't point the gun at me, there's no need for that.

OK, I admit it, I talk too much, and I always like to have the last word.

+++++

Go on then, leave. See if I care. But before you go, can you teach me how to burn salad?

No, I don't suppose it was that goddamn funny.

I'm sorry. There, I've said it. Are you happy now?

BANG (collapses)

(wife shouts from audience) Yes!

Goldilocks and the Three Bears

CHAV STYLE

'You 'eard wot I sez, Dwayne, get yer own Bacardi Breezer yeah; coz I'm gonna read our bay-bee a bedtime story, you get me?'

'Waynetta, this story is about a bird called Goldilocks.'

'Wot sorta name's that?'

'Dunno, sounds chavvy to me. Anyroad, in her Burberry trakkie, Nike trainers and bling, she looked proper mint as she skipped through the woods. Then she found a cottage with the door open and decided to ponce a drink. She shouts "hello", but no-one's home, so she goes in, right, and in the kitchen finds three bowls of porridge. She eats from the first bowl but it's too hot, innit; and the second one's too cold.'

'Urrgh! Cold porridge. That's gross.'

'But the third bowl waz just right so she wolfs it dahn, then she's like, tired, and decides to catch some zzz's. The first two chair's she sits on are too big, innit; but the third one's boss, you get me; so she leans back, put's her Nike-covered feet on the table – and the chair breaks. She's totally gobsmacked, innit? The thing is, right, she's really tired now, so she goes upstairs for a lie dahn, but the first bed she tried was too hard.'

'I know that feelin', this bed's too 'ard.'

'Stop dissin' me, yeah? Show some respect to your

muvva. I'm on the dole, innit. You gotta roof over your head, dontcha? So Goldilocks finds the second bed too 'ard, but the third bed was mint – an' she falls asleep, innit. Then, the three bears return home; and it all kicks off, yeah?'

'"Someone's bin eating my porridge," sez daddy bear.'

'"Someone's bin eating my porridge," sez mommy bear.

'"Someone's bin eating my porridge," sez the bay-bee, "and they ate the lot."

'So they goes in the next room, yeah? "Someone's been in my chair," sez daddy bear.'

'How'd he know?'

'I dunno? Maybe she left her trakkie on it, oright? Jeez, it's only a mingin' bedtime story. "Someone's been in my chair," sez mommy bear. "Someone's been in my chair," sez the bay-bee, "an' they broke it."

'So they go upstairs, right, searching for a burglar. "Someone's been sleepin' in my bed," sez daddy bear. "Someone's been sleepin' in my bed," sez mommy bear.'

'Why don't they sleep togevva?'

'I dunno; maybe he snores? Anyroad, the bay-bee finds Goldilocks asleep in her bed, and daddy bear starts givin' it large. "Whatchadoin' in our gaff?" and Goldilocks wakes up surrounded, so she shouts: "Watchoolookinat? You neva seen a chav before?" Then she legs it dahn the path into the woods. An' that's the Goldilocks story, innit?'

'Wicked! Now will you tell me about Jack and the beanstalk, an' that chicken that lays the gold bling?'

'Tommorra, if you behave; else I won't bovva; you get me?'

PERFORMANCE POETRY, i.e. performed
with movement and expression

Some Things
Never Leave You

The memories of family holidays,
are a source of strength for me,
as I look back on the old days;
we were always very happy.

My two (or was it three?) brothers,
and me - whatsits - ma and pa;
we'd all pile in the thingy with four wheels,
(clicks fingers) *got it; the family motor car.*

I can't remember the make of it,
Morris? Ford? Cabriolet?
But we always ended up in a thingy,
like a hut, you know; got it, a chalet.

There were these tall trees,
and that green stuff, grass,
and we played that sport with a bat,
not cricket, soft balls; (clicks fingers), *tennis.*

I liked to eat that stuff in buns,
you know, burgers and cheeseburgers;
and ice on a stick, yes, lollipops,
and ice cream, in wafers.

The sky was blue, no fluffy clouds,
and it never rained, you know;
and that red thing in the sky - the sun,
it was always hot; we never had snow.

There was this big bloke with us;
(clicks fingers) *I know who it was, it was me dad;*
and we swam in a whatsit, a swimming pool,
they were the happiest times I ever had.

There was a hairy, smelly thing with ears;
not a horse, (clicks fingers) *a donkey.*
I didn't, yes I did, I rode it once,
and me legs went kind of wonky.

I was really scared of that one thing -
runs on a track (scratches head)*, the ghost train;*
with what spiders make (clicks fingers) *cobwebs.*
It's all right here, you know, in me brain.

It's like it was only – not tomorrow – yesterday.
Those memories are very clear, it's true,
of those happy family outings;
I guess some things never leave you.

+++++

First Love

At the age of 16, Jake Wilson had been strong, good looking, and popular at school, but in order for him to stay popular, other people had to suffer, and Susan Richards had been asking for it. She had followed him around like a lovesick puppy, making it so easy for him to lead her on, much to the amusement of his followers. He had built up her hopes by promising to take her to the prom, and then dumped her for Sophie Baxter. Sophie was more his type; she was ready, willing and able, whereas Susan was unready, unwilling, and easily squashed.

He had thought he knew everything back then, but looking back, he realised that he had known nothing. If he could change one thing from his past, it would be the way that he dumped her at the prom.

Jake flicked the stack of six beer mats into the air with the back of his hand, catching them between his thumb and fingers. He increased the stack of beer mats to ten. 'What are my chances?'

Lenny, his partner-in-crime from their schooldays, weighed up the odds. 'Slim, just like your chances of meeting Susan Richards at tonight's school reunion.'

Jake flicked the beer mats up with the back of his hand, and sent them flying across the table, failing to catch any. 'I wonder what she's doing now?'

'Not pining for you, mate; that's for sure. She's probably married with three ankle-biters.'

'Do you think so?'

'Course I don't. Last thing I 'eard, she'd tried to top herself.'

'Don't say that, Lenny, it's not funny.'
'Who's joking?'

At the age of 16, Susan Richards had been a certifiable romantic. She couldn't remember a time in her life when she wasn't 'in love' or with a crush on someone. She idolised relationships, foolishly looked past faults, and attached her heart to someone far too quickly.

As she sat at her dressing table, she remembered the day that she saw her first true love. Jake Wilson strode through the school gates on the 14th of September 2002, pushing smaller pupils aside. His jet black hair shone in the sunlight; his face was so enigmatic, so irresistible, that she fell in love with him immediately. She remembered the first time he held her in his arms behind the bike sheds, and she remembered his pale green eyes as he stole his first kiss.

Rubbing moisturising cream into her scarred wrists, she recalled the night of the school prom, the day her first true love ripped her heart out and trampled her hopes and dreams into dust. She was fragile back then, fragile and delicate, but he callously destroyed her in front of the whole school. She remembered arriving home in her tear-stained dress, reduced from princess to pauper by Jake Wilson, to find her mother battered and bruised, and her father gone. Her whole life ruined.

Brenda slid out of bed and began massaging Susan's neck and shoulders. 'You don't have to go, Suzie, come back to bed.'

'Oh yes I do. I need to hurt him like he hurt me.'

'You've come so far during the last two turbulent years; the last thing you need is another spell inside.'

They hugged in silence for a while, as Susan ran through what she might say to Jake and what he might say to her. 'For my plan to work, Brenda, I need to look my best; please help me choose an outfit.'

The trauma of her public humiliation and the divorce of her parents drove Susan into a deep depression. Unable to face people, she found her own flat and moved away. She started sleeping around, just to feel loved again, and this led to prostitution, two police cautions and a spell inside, culminating with her attempted suicide.

Her cell-mate Brenda, serving time for aggravated burglary, found Susan just in time, saving her life, and their friendship began, especially when Brenda learned that Susan had a place to live. Once on the outside, they became lovers. At last, Susan felt wanted again. Their mutual hatred of men became their common bond, and the unlikely duo plotted Susan's revenge. There were two options: Brenda favoured luring Jake to a quiet place to castrate him, but Susan favoured leading him on, all the way to the altar, where *she* would dump *him*.

Outside the school, seated in Brenda's car, Susan pointed him out. 'That's Jake.'

Brenda was not impressed. 'Are you sure you're strong enough to do this?'

'Only because I have you for back-up.'

Brenda fingered the knife in the specially-made sheath inside her denim jacket as she watched from the car.

Susan crossed the road and paused at the school gates as memories came flooding back.

'Susan, is that you?' She turned to see Jake rushing towards her: an older Jake, whose black hair had lost some of its shine, but he was obviously still full of his own self importance. 'Susan, how have you been?'

For some inexplicable reason, her heart skipped a beat. 'And what's it got to do with you?'

Jake looked her up and down. 'Susan, I expect you to be angry with me. Lord knows, I deserve it. I'm sorry that I treated you so badly.'

'How is Sophie bloody Baxter, anyway?'

'I haven't seen her for years. Let me buy you a drink; there's a bar and disco inside the school hall.'

'I'm not going inside; too many bad memories. I came here to draw a line through the past. Now it's time for me to move on, but don't let me stop you; there's bound to be someone in there you can bully.'

She turned to walk away, but Jake grabbed her hand, his touch spreading warmth through her body. From the car, Brenda fingered her knife, watching him closely.

'Susan. I've waited five years for the opportunity to say sorry. There's a pub over there; at least give me five minutes to apologise.'

She removed her hand from his. This was going to be much easier than she had thought. 'OK, five minutes, but it had better be good.'

At a discreet distance, Brenda followed them into the nearby pub.

For five years, Susan's disappearance had haunted Jake. Part of him hoped that the attempted suicide rumours were untrue, and that she had settled down and was now married with kids. Another part of him wondered if he had been so busy staying popular that he had missed a chance of true love.

Susan supped her orange juice. 'Come on then; the clock is ticking. Say what you have to say.'

'I've changed, Susan. I've done some growing up.'

'Is that it?'

He reached for her hand and turned it to expose her wrist. 'So it's true?' Susan pulled her sleeve back over her scars. Jake's eyes began to fill with tears. He needed a moment to compose himself. 'I'm so sorry for the hurt I've caused you. Please give me a minute; I'll be right back.'

Once alone, she wrote her phone number on a slip of paper, slipped it under his pint, and left.

Back in the flat, Brenda poured two glasses of wine as Susan's phone beeped again. 'It looks like he's hooked, Suzie; how many messages is that?'

'I've lost count. All I have to do now is slowly reel him in, and then I can rip his guts out.'

Brenda put Susan's phone on mute and pulled her onto the bed. 'Or we could just castrate him?'

Lenny smiled when he saw Jake enter the Kings Head. 'You were quick, I told you she wouldn't turn up.'

'Oh, she turned up, *and* we talked, but I turned my back for a second and she ran out on me.'

'Time to move on then, mate; I'll get the beers in.'

While Lenny was at the bar, Jake sent another text. He wasn't ready to move on just yet. Susan had aroused feelings in him, but were they caused by guilt?

After he'd sent her 36 text messages in three days, Susan agreed to meet him again. He offered to pick her up, but she declined, preferring to keep her present whereabouts a secret. The less he knew about her, the easier it would be to leave him with a broken heart.

During their first shared meal and with a couple of pints inside him, Jake began to take more notice of her little black dress, her sultry brown eyes and her inviting red lips. She looked far more attractive now than she ever had at school. Jake tried to re-open the past so that he could justify his actions. 'Back then, I wasn't really...'

Susan stopped him. 'The past has gone, Jake; I'm only interested in the future.'

'And could your future include me?'

She kept him dangling for a few moments, before giving an encouraging smile. 'Who knows? Stranger things have happened.'

At the end of the evening, Jake decided to kiss her. It was risky, and certainly too soon, but he needed to test his feelings.

Although taken by surprise, Susan allowed him his moment on her lips, before pushing him away. 'It's too soon, I'm not sure I'm ready.'

As a waitress cleared their table, Jake slyly gave her figure the once over, before returning his attention to Susan, who was seriously considering Brenda's plan to castrate him.

'Susan, there's no hurry; let's just take things one step at a time.' Jake was besotted, totally taken in by her fragility, and the kiss had left him wanting more.

Ex-prostitute Susan used all of her expertise to keep Jake interested, and managed to keep him at arm's length, but it wasn't easy. There were times when she wanted to be ravished by this man who clearly loved her, she longed to be loved and cherished, but no. As Brenda kept reminding her, the bastard had to pay.

One evening, he noticed that she was wearing stockings, and she explained that, as she was beginning to trust him, she had started to relax and feel more like a woman. When he became impatient and frustrated, she would gently remind him that he had said 'there's no hurry', and slowly, but surely, using all the tricks of the trade, she reeled in her catch.

Lenny almost dropped his pint. 'You did what?'

'I proposed to Susan, and she accepted. We're getting married next week. Will you be my best man?'

'Isn't this a bit sudden? You've only been seeing her for two months. She's not even your type.'

'Is that a yes or a no?'

'Well, if you insist; I wouldn't want to miss this for the world.'

The following week, Jake and Lenny were drinking in the Kings Head. 'Not much of a stag night, is it, Jake, just me and you?'

'Susan wanted to keep it low-key. Only a few people know about the wedding.'

'Doesn't that seem strange to you?'

'Not really; she can't handle stress.'

A few beers later, Lenny just had to ask: 'So, is she good in bed?' Jake glanced down at his pint. 'You haven't slept with her? That's typical of you; always chasing what you can't have. This isn't love; she isn't even your type. I can't believe you're marrying the class nerd.'

Jake returned home and opened a bottle of scotch. The more he drank, the stronger his doubts grew. What if Lenny was right? Could he break her heart, again?

Susan's hen night also consisted of two people. Brenda had never given away anything in her life, and the last thing she wanted to give away was Susan, but after many tears and tantrums, she decided that if she *did* agree to give Susan away, at least she would be on hand to ensure that Jake got his just deserts.

By the time they arrived home, they were arguing again. Brenda needed some space, and stormed out the flat shouting, 'Don't bother to wait up!'

Susan sat in front of her dressing table and poured herself a drink. She realised that tomorrow, if she said, 'I don't,' it would break Jake's heart, and if she said, 'I do,' it would break Brenda's heart.

Saying 'I do' was never meant to be on the agenda, but tonight in the pub, all she could see were people 'in love'. The whispered sweet-nothings, the seductive smiles, the holding of hands, it had been all around her. Romance was what she truly longed for, but she knew that she would never get it from Brenda. Her whole life was one gigantic mess. She poured herself another Jack Daniel's. Two hearts were on the line. Which one should she break? She was confused, the pressure was too much. She stared once more at the razor-blade, and took another drink.

With sirens and headlights blazing, the ambulance raced through red traffic lights. It was a matter of life and death. Inside the ambulance, the blood-splattered paramedic tried to stem the flow of blood from the multiple wounds.

The registry office staff checked their watches. They could leave it another five minutes, before Jake Wilson and Susan Richards would have to arrange another date. Often, the bride or the groom was late, but not usually both of them.

A taxi finally pulled up outside the registry office, and out stepped Susan, radiant in a pink suit and matching hat. Brenda, dressed in a cream outfit, led her into the registry office, where she checked Susan's bandages.

Every time the door swung open, Susan's heart quickened, and every time it wasn't Jake, her heart broke a little more.

Lenny finally appeared in the waiting room. 'Is Jake here? I can't find him anywhere and he's not answering his phone.'

Susan was too upset to utter a word, so Brenda answered on her behalf. 'No, he isn't here. Looks like he's broken her heart again.'

After two days in bed, cared for by Brenda, Susan felt strong enough to get up. She checked her phone, still no messages. She called Jake again, still no answer. She threw her phone across the room.

'Men, they all need castrating,' said Brenda. 'I'm going for a shower.'

Susan shuffled into the kitchen to put the kettle on, and noticed Brenda's stained denim jacket in the laundry basket.

'Brenda, Brenda?' she shouted urgently.

Brenda poked her head out the bathroom door. 'Keep your hair on, Suzie. What's so important that it won't wait until I've had my shower?'

Susan held up the jacket. 'Whose blood is this?'

+++++

182

Never Again!

Was it peer pressure that made me do it, or stupidity?

The popular ones had said they could avoid doing it, and my twisted logic said, if I avoided doing it, I'd become popular just like them, but this was not my idea of fun, I can't hold out much longer. I have never gone so long without doing it.

I started doing it at a young age, and soon got into trouble at school. I do it everywhere I go. I do it on trains, in elevators, and once, just to help pass the time on a transatlantic flight, I did it for four hours, much to the annoyance of passengers who were trying to sleep.

Earlier, I was tempted to do it with Jason; I know he loves doing it too, but Liz was watching us closely, not that she could tell on us, I reasoned. She would have had to keep quiet.

I like to do it with strangers when I'm on holiday, and sometimes, I do it with my sister. My girlfriend said she once caught me doing it in my sleep, and when we do it together, I often let her go first; she likes that. But for now, I must keep it zipped. Some mornings, I've even done it in bed with God.

I'm desperate to do it now.

A loud whistle pierced the quiet, and cheers filled the hall at the announcement: 'The sponsored silence is over –you can now talk.'

Never again!

The Day of Rapture

'Bill, I was just watching live football on TV and my team were awarded a penalty against Manchester United at Old Trafford. Now that was a miracle in itself, but as we took it, the United goalie disappeared in a puff of smoke, along with two full-backs, a midfielder and two forwards. I was shocked, I can tell you, it was unbelievable. We hadn't scored at United for 31 years.

'So I shouted for Doris to come out from the kitchen and see, but she's vanished as well. All that's left are two marigolds, an apron, a nun's habit and a half-prepared Sunday dinner, and it's suddenly gone all dark.'

'Yeah, same here. I reckon there's a storm brewing. Can you hear trumpets playing?'

'Yes I can; it's not Children In Need again, is it?'

'Don't think so.'

'There's only one explanation then. I think she's been "raptured".'

'I didn't know your missus had got religion.'

'Nor me. Apart from hanging a cross in every room, annual pilgrimages to the Vatican, and wearing a nun's habit every Sunday, she showed no signs of religion whatsoever. Quick, Bill, put your TV on, there's a newsflash.'

From Buckingham Palace, Camilla addressed the nation. 'Most members of the royal family seem to have disappeared, but don't panic, I've taken charge of the UK, and I've spoken to Hilary Clinton at the White

House. Until they find someone from the Obama family, she's taken charge of America.' As Camilla spoke, her complexion began turning red, and horns grew bigger and bigger on her head.

'Bill, are you watching? Camilla's looking hornier by the minute.'

'I can't believe you've just said that Stan; your missus has only been gone five minutes.'

'Is that all it is, five minutes? Blimey, I'm missing the old trout already. Did I ever tell you, Doris's cooking melted in me mouth, after a couple of hours.'

'Come to think of it, Stan, if it is the day of rapture, and all good people have gone to heaven, was I the first person you phoned?'

'Well, yes.'

'So you assumed that I'd still be here?'

That was a tricky one to answer. 'It wasn't like that, mate, honest, I phoned you because you're my best mate. By the way, is your missus still around?'

'What do you think?'

Now that was a tricky one, also. 'Bill, I can't imagine Elsie would ever leave you, mate,' was the best answer he could come up with at such short notice.

'Yeah, she's still here, Stan.'

'Great news, Bill. I'm really pleased for you, mate. Can I come round for Sunday lunch?'

Based on an idea by Nick Page

+++++

Out of Retirement

In the sprawling metropolis of Gottem City, Commissioner Graham and Chief O'Hairy surveyed the damage.

'Who could have done this dastardly crime Chief O'Hairy? Who could have stolen all the toilets and left us with nothing to go on?'

'But we do have something to go on, sir.'

'Oh good,' sighed a relieved commissioner, 'I need to go now.'

'No sir, I mean we have a clue to go on: the graffiti on the wall.' Both heads turned in unison to read the message painted on the toilet wall. *The Miss Universe pageant is fixed. All the winners are from earth.*

'There's only one thing for it,' said Commissioner Graham, wiping cobwebs off the bat-phone; 'there's only one team that can solve this crime, Bratman and Robbin.'

'But sir, haven't they been retired for almost ten years?'

Billionaire Bruce Waine dozed in his rocking chair, the top button of his trousers undone to make room for his stomach that had spread through ten years of inactivity. His not-so-young ward Dick Gayson was in better shape, having joined a squash club with friends. Every Saturday they would club together and buy a bottle of squash.

'Bruce old chum, why don't you join me on this new whisky diet?'

'Is it any good?'

'I'll say. I've already lost four days. Holy cryptic clues, Bruce, these crosswords are getting tougher. To egg on, five letters, starts with a t and ends with a t.'

Bruce Waine closed his eyes and thought back to the good old days, when his expertise was valued. 'Two egg on, five letters? I think you'll find the answer is toast.'

With the help of a zimmer frame, Alfie the butler clunked into the room. 'Master Waine,' he croaked, 'I do believe the brat-phone is ringing.'

Dick, the more athletic of the undynamic duo, reached the phone first, just as it stopped ringing. Gasping for breath, Bruce Waine hit the recall button.

'I'll put it on hands-free, Dick, so that you can listen.' After three rings, the call was answered.

'Thank you for calling the Commissioner's Office; calls may be recorded for training and monitoring purposes. Please press one for opening hours, two for the press secretary, three for the Commissioner, and four to hear these options again.'

Dick pressed three. 'Hello, commissioner?'

'Hello,' replied the commissioner, 'are you Robbin?'

'No, I live here.' *(Think about it – Ed).*

Bruce Waine grabbed the phone. 'Good morning commissioner, how can we be of service?'

'Bratman, we need your help. Gottem City is under threat from the world's most dangerous team.'

'You don't mean . . . Wimbledon Football Club?'

'No Bratman, worse than that.'

'Worse than Wimbledon? You don't mean . . . Millwall?'

'No, Bratman; it's your old enemies, the Graffiti Brothers.'

Bruce Waine sucked in his stomach and puffed out his chest. This was a chance to show they weren't past it. 'Commissioner, we'll be right over.' He turned to Dick. 'Come on, to the brat-poles.'

(Sing) dada dada dada dada dada dada dada dada, Bratman. (stop singing).

'But Bratman, we had the rusty brat-poles removed two years ago.'

'OK, forget the brat-poles, we'll use the stairs. Alfie, have you seen my tights?'

Ten minutes later, they reached the Bratmobile. Robbin jumped into his seat, but Bratman, whose costume was straining at the seams, gingerly slid behind the steering wheel before turning the ignition. Nothing happened. He tried again. Nothing. 'Robbin, I think the battery's flat.'

'Holy complications Bratman, what shape should it be?'

Bratman slid out of the car. 'Robbin, to the brat-cave.'

'Do you have a plan already? Gee, that was quick.'

'No Robbin; I've split my tights.'

While Bratman changed his tights, Robbin thought back to their last encounter with the Graffiti Brothers who had tortured them with: *save the Earth, it's the only planet with chocolate; conserve toilet paper, use both sides; and save a tree, eat a beaver.*

'Robbin,' called Bratman from the changing rooms, 'what are these magazines doing in your locker?'

Robbin blushed. 'Bratman, er, I can explain.'

'I can't believe you have magazines like these.'

'Holy superheroes Bratman, if they upset you that much, I'll destroy my Spiderman magazines.'

Two hours later, with the car fully charged, they were on their way.

(Sing) dada dada dada dada dada dada dada dada, Bratman. (stop singing).

The Bratmobile skidded to a halt outside the commissioner's office and they struggled upstairs to survey the damaged toilets.

'Are you sure you're up to this challenge?' asked a concerned commissioner, noticing Bratman's beer belly.

'Oh this is just protective covering for my rock-hard abs,' said Bratman, wobbling his belly up and down, 'I suspect the Graffiti Brothers plan to disrupt the Miss America Contest.'

'Holy pageants, Bratman,' said Robbin. 'Why do we choose from 50 people for Miss America, but only two people for president?'

'A good question, Robbin; but we have criminals to catch. Commissioner, where were the Graffiti Brothers last seen?'

'In Artifact Avenue, near the city museum.'

Bratman twirled his cape like a matador, and it tangled around his legs. 'Robbin, we have no time to lose.' He untangled his cape. 'To the Bratmobile.'

(Sing) dada dada dada dada dada dada dada dada, Bratman. (stop singing).

They returned to street level to find a traffic officer issuing a ticket.

'Officer, what seems to be the problem?'

'Parking over designated white lines and occupying two parking spaces is a traffic violation with a $40 fine.'

'Holy political correctness,' said Robbin, 'don't you know who we are?'

Easy Robbin,' said Bratman holding him back, he's probably not seen us before.'

Bratman jumped into the Bratmobile, fired up the engine, opened his window, and took the ticket. 'Thank you officer for your diligence. I will pay this fine within the required 14 days.'

As they pulled away from the sidewalk in a cloud of smoke, the officer shouted after them. 'And get your exhaust fixed.'

(Sing) dada dada dada dada dada dada dada dada, Bratman. (Stop singing).

They skidded sideways to a halt outside the city museum, and caught the Graffiti Brothers red-handed as they painted, *never accept a drink from a urologist.*

Bratman shouted, 'Stick your hands up ya bums.' *(Hey, you can't say that, this is family reading. Ed).*

A vicious fight ensued. POW, Bratman punched one of the Graffiti Brothers. KAPOW, Robbin threw another onto the floor. ZAPP, Bratman threw another punch; but the out-of-condition undynamic duo soon grew tired.

Robbin was trapped in a corner. 'Hey, Robbin, does this smell like chloroform?' Robbin was quickly rendered unconscious. SPLATT, a large net fell onto Bratman and he too was overpowered with the use of chloroform.

The undynamic duo regained consciousness in an underground cave somewhere outside the city; and found themselves tied back-to-back, and positioned between giant speakers.

'Robbin, my trusty sidekick, can you reach the ear-plugs in my brat-belt?'

'No, my hands are well and truly tied. Can you reach your homing device to alert Alfie?'

'I'll try, but these ropes are extremely tight.'

Near the cave entrance, the Graffiti Brothers, holding microphones, looked down on them. One opened a stop-cock and water began filling the cave.

'We've got you now,' they mocked, their voices booming through the loudspeakers, 'we're going to chant graffiti messages at you until you drown.'

Robbin struggled harder as water washed around his feet. 'Holy mental torture Bratman.'

'Easy, my faithful sidekick, easy.'

The torture began. *Gun control is a steady hand; if Barbie is so popular, why do you have to buy her friends?* They twisted in pain as water rose to knee-high. *Jesus is coming, look busy; rehab is for quitters; relish today, ketchup tomorrow.*

Will the undynamic duo escape from this torture? Will Bratman pay his parking ticket? Will DC Comics sue me for breach of copyright? Is anyone still reading this? Tune in next week. Listening to the radio has to be better than reading this.

All together now: (Sing) dada dada dada dada dada dada dada dada, Bratman (stop singing).

+++++

Don't Count Your Chickens

I would rather listen to a Yoko Ono CD than my wife's snoring, I thought, as I waited for her to wake up. Marriage kills passion because after the ceremony, you're sleeping with a relative. Mind you, she's creative in bed, I'll give her that. She does word-searches, crosswords *and* Sudoku. She turned over and grunted, as if to say you can think what you like, I'm not waking up yet. I gave up waiting, trudged downstairs, put the kettle on, and searched the house, but my present was harder to find than Tony Blair's scruples.

I returned to the kitchen empty-handed, and as the kettle boiled, I felt two hands snake around my waist and clutch what used to be my six-pack.

'Guess who?'

'If that's Katie Price, I've told you before, we need to be discreet, my wife's upstairs.'

My wife slapped my pyjama-covered bottom. 'Please come back to bed.'

'Why? Can't you finish the crossword? Here's a clue: one word, eight letters, celebrated once a year.'

'Christmas?'

'Try again.'

'New year's day?'

'That's three words.'

'Whitsun?'

'Now you're being silly.'

She put her hands to her face in mock horror. 'Oh no, I've forgotten the birthday of my awfully-wedded husband.'

'No you haven't. Where is it?'

She stole my newly made cup of tea and took a sip. 'I'll give you your present if you get back in bed.'

'Now you're talking.' I vaulted the stairs, three at a time.

'Now, close your eyes and hold out your hands.'

My shaking hands gripped the present tightly, my heart beating fast. I had been dropping hints about the book I wanted for the last three weeks, now at last, I held it in my hands. I tore frantically at the wrapping paper, and there it was...... not.

'What's this, *A Beginner's Guide to Poultry Keeping?* This isn't the book I wanted!' Then I noticed the ill-fitted dust jacket.

My wife smiled. 'Gottcha!'

Underneath the false jacket was *African Adventures of a Born-Again Atheist.* As I began to read the back cover, my wife climbed back into bed. 'Now do want your second present?'

'Haven't you got a crossword to do, dear? Can't you see I'm busy?'

+++++

Forever Blue *(and white)*

My football team aren't very good,
You may not know their name.
I'd like to change them if I could,
And begin all over again.

From West Brom to Manchester United,
The change would be easy to do.
They'd certainly win a lot more games,
But I'm a Baggie through and through.

So you can keep the Champion's League,
Wayne Rooney, Giggs and Fergie,
I think I'll stay just as I am,
A boing, boing, Baggie.

We bounce between the Premier League,
And the Championship below,
In 1968 we won the FA Cup,
But that was 43 years ago.

It's my solemn duty to soldier on,
Through thick and thin and thinner.
Wives may come and wives may go,
But your football team remain forever.

Up the Baggies!

Pushy Mums

The air is heavy with the smell of sweat and the sound of grunting and heaving. 'I can't go on.' I protest, but a chorus of encouragement from those around me spurs me on.

'Push,' a voice yells, and I do, straining so hard, I feel the veins in my neck stand out, and more sweat rolls down my back. 'Come on, keep pushing,' the voice yells again.

'I can't go on, I'm exhausted. I need a break, preferably with a banana milkshake and a large slice of strawberry cheesecake.'

'Keep pushing, you're almost there,' the voice orders, so I strain some more, aching now in places where I never knew I had muscles.

'My baby's far too big, I can't do this,' I gasp, and after a crescendo of panting, thankfully, we stop for a rest.

My seven-month old daughter squawks at me as I collapse on the grass beside her buggy. Together with ten other mothers, I begin stretching my aching muscles; that is until I see my giggling daughter waving to me as her buggy rolls down the hill towards the main road. I haven't moved that fast since my husband came home with an Indian takeaway.

I wonder if I will I ever regain my pre-pregnancy figure.

Snippets follow from the comedy adventure:
AFRICAN ADVENTURES OF
A BORN-AGAIN ATHEIST

Foreword

I dare you to enter Brian's World, and if you do, be ready for the unexpected and take your sense of humour along. Brian will hook you from page one with his incredible yarn about Jack Daniel's, Kenyan toilets, atheism, God, tomato sauce, nightmares and conversations with born-again Christians. This is a real story, a true adventure - I laughed out loud in places but was also moved by his stories of faith and compassion in Africa.

Brian is larger than life and Brian's World is a place of humour, honesty, fear, courage, faith and a God who doesn't pull his punches. It's quite a place to be.

Please read this, enjoy it and let it affect you. You may end up wanting to go round the world, you may not. But you will I am sure hear the voice of God whispering to you.

Dave Hopwood, Author of The Bloke's Bible.

Although *African Adventures of a Born-Again Atheist* is light-hearted, the situation in Africa is deadly serious. Therefore, all profits from this book will go to help Kenyan widows and orphans. To view photos & video, please visit www.brianhumphreys.co.uk. Thank you.

If Jesus Returned Today

That night I had a strange dream that Jesus came back to earth and made himself known in London. Millions of people caused chaos at airports around the world as they tried to secure tickets to Heathrow and there was pandemonium at French ports as all ships across the Channel became oversubscribed. The cost of flights (and ferries from France) doubled, pound shops brought out a multitude of cheap religious artefacts and, of course, Piers Morgan got to interview him first.

Sky outbid everyone for the TV rights, and these were some of the questions fired at him: where have you been? Can you save the planet? Can you do something about lowering the price of petrol? Americans via a satellite link had their own set of important questions. How did Barack Obama get elected? If an African elephant moves to the States, does it become an African-American elephant? Can you drive a hearse containing a body in the carpool lane? And David Attenborough asked Jesus, 'why did you put the kneecaps of a flamingo on backwards?'

Jesus tried to escape the crowds by boat on the River Thames, but the paparazzi in private helicopters, hot air balloons and hang gliders hounded him everywhere he went. Hundreds of pregnant women came forward claiming they were pregnant by the Holy Spirit and *You've Been Framed* had a special programme with video clips of the Almighty.

Newspapers offered thousands of pounds for mobile phone snaps, and posters on the side of London buses declared what millions of Christians around the world had been saying: 'There IS a God and we told you so!' Simon Cowell changed the name of his programme to *Britain's Got God-given Talent*, and asked Jesus to be a judge.

The *Sun* newspaper changed its allegiance once again. After ditching Labour for the Conservatives, it now ditched the Conservatives and rebranded itself as the *Messenger* – voice of the chosen people. A 36-page souvenir edition explained how the editor had had visions and prophesised that this day would come. Mystic Meg announced her retirement and page three girls were made redundant.

For every person filled with love and hope, there were others filled with hate. Suicide bombers and religious fanatics (and people of great wealth who did not fancy the idea of a sharing, caring world) were out to get him.

Facebook, Twitter and all social network sites went into meltdown as the following jokes were sent around the world: what car would Jesus drive? A Christler. What would Jesus tweet? Smacked my thumb with a hammer today, it hurts like the devil. What would Jesus eat? Definitely a low-calorie balanced diet... have you seen the Lord's abs?

Where would he stay? Who would look after him? Who would pour Victoria Beckham perfume on his feet? Would taxi drivers charge him double like most foreigners?

The 'poster boys' of Africa (Gaddafi, Mugabe and Zuma) were shaking at the knees and locked themselves inside their diamond-encrusted, gold-plated palaces, and the poor around the world sank to their knees and rejoiced in prayer.

One of my mum's mantras came to mind as I woke from the dream in a cold, cold sweat. She always warned me to behave, because on judgment day all of my sins would be replayed on a giant screen for all to see. All of my wrong-doing - in high definition - on a giant plasma screen - in 3D. Ouch!

+++++

A Visit to Hell

'Welcome home,' said the devil. 'Leave your helmet of salvation at the door; the Jack Daniel's is on me. Welcome to my non-prophet organisation.' Laughter burst out from the shadows and I took another drink. The background music was *Bat out of Hell*.

'So tell me, how was Africa?' asked the devil.

'Corrupt.'

I took another drink. My eyes were drawn to the large plasma screen showing pornography on the far wall. I tried not to look, but the temptation was too strong.

'You've been in Africa for a while; what have you learned?' prompted the devil.

I took another drink. 'That my prayers only get answered if I forward an email to seven of my friends and make a wish within five minutes. Otherwise a large pigeon with diarrhoea lands on my head.'

'If it's any consolation,' laughed the devil, 'I always send my favourite pigeon.'

'Who cares about Africa?' said a voice from the shadows. 'Let's play a game. Why is a drink better than

Jesus?'

'You don't need to wait 2,000 years for another drink,' said the devil. Cheers rang out from the shadows.

Another voice: 'A drink doesn't tell you how to have sex.'

'There are laws saying a drinks label cannot lie to you,' said another.

'You can prove you have a beer,' I said, taking another drink. Laughter filled the room and the background music changed to *Sympathy for the Devil*.

I raised my glass. 'My name is Brian, I love alcohol and I'm not saved. It has been six days since my last prayer and quite frankly, my dear, I don't give a damn.' Laughter filled the room once more.

'Welcome home,' said the devil. 'Let's play some poker.'

Through the night, we drank and played Texas Hold'em with a deck of tarot cards. I got a royal flush and five people died.

+++++

Lightning Source UK Ltd.
Milton Keynes UK
UKOW050843240812

198013UK00001B/35/P